# HIRED BY THE
# MYSTERIOUS
# MILLIONAIRE

# HIRED BY THE MYSTERIOUS MILLIONAIRE

ALLY BLAKE

MILLS & BOON

First published in Great Britain 2019
by Mills & Boon, an imprint of HarperCollins*Publishers*
1 London Bridge Street, London, SE1 9GF

Large Print edition 2019

© 2019 Ally Blake

ISBN: 978-0-263-08245-6

**MIX**
Paper from
responsible sources
**FSC® C007454**

This book is produced from independently certified
FSC™ paper to ensure responsible forest management. For
more information visit www.harpercollins.co.uk/green.

Printed and bound in Great Britain
by CPI Group (UK) Ltd, Croydon, CR0 4YY

The seed of this story came to me fifteen years ago and would not have survived had I not written it down. Therefore I dedicate this book to the scraps of paper, backs of receipts and many beautiful notebooks that have given themselves over to my career.

# CHAPTER ONE

"IT'S HIM. It has to be."

Ignoring her friend's imploring voice, Evie Croft let her body rock with the soothing motion of the morning train as it rumbled along the Frankston Line. Swiping through the ads in the Room Rent app, she tried really hard to feel enthused about exorbitant rent, alarming-sounding housemates, or both.

"Evie!" Zoe whispered, loudly enough that the schoolboys sitting across from them actually looked up from their phones. "You know who I mean. He's nose-deep in a book the size of a house brick, so you can look. *Look.* Look *now.*"

Evie knew Zoe was talking about her "train boyfriend" and she had no intention of looking. She'd already accidentally made eye contact with Hot Stuff in the Swanky Suit today, and many more times since he'd started taking her train.

It was hard not to. With his overlong hair and rugged stubble, the man was a study in the kind of dark, broody countenance you just couldn't fake.

"Stop looking at that stupid app," said Zoe.

"You are not moving out of my apartment just because Lance is moving in and that's final."

Evie gave her oldest friend a squeezy one-armed hug. "I love you because you truly believe it. You and Lance have been waiting for this moment since you were sixteen years old. He's home from deployment next week and it's finally happening."

Zoe sat back, closed her eyes and sighed. "It really is, isn't it?"

Either way, Evie gave up on looking for a new place to stay. Only half an hour out from the biggest job interview of her life—with Game Plan, no less, a coder's Holy Grail—she instead practised answering interview questions in her head.

At least, she tried. Until Zoe leaned over, reaching for her phone. "Click back to that other app. No, the other one. Go back."

"Gah!" Evie held her phone up high, out in front, then opened the neck of her top and slipped her phone between sternum and bra.

Zoe cocked an eyebrow. "You really think that's going to stop me?"

Evie did not. With only a super-quick glance in the direction of Hot Stuff in the Swanky Suit to make sure he wasn't watching, she dug beneath her vintage pea coat and warm winter top to fish out her phone, shivering as her chilly fingers grazed her skin. And rocking into the older man sardined in beside her. She sent him an apologetic smile. The barest flicker of his cheek was a tale of eternal sufferance.

The train commute took all sorts. The bored schoolkids, the frazzled mums with toddlers and prams in tow, women in piercings leaning on men with tattoos, creative office types with their smooth hair and manicured nails. It was a delicious microcosm of the city at large.

Evie had grown up in a small dairy community, just north of Echuca, and her favourite memory of her mother was listening to her wax lyrical about the short time she'd lived in Melbourne—the electric hum of creativity, the eclectic fashion, the epicurean delights. She remembered tracing the delicate "Adventure" tattoo etched into her mother's fine wrist.

After her mum died Evie had promised herself she'd end up there one day too and have the life her mother had never had.

Though the past couple of weeks the city had been making her work for it.

"Seriously?" Evie cried when Zoe whipped her phone away with a delighted, "Aha! Now, let's see what Hot Stuff in the Swanky Suit has to say."

Zoe didn't mean "in person". For she and Hot Stuff had never had an actual conversation.

Well, unless you counted that first day. She'd made it to the train doors right as they'd pulled up to their city stop when the train had lurched to a halt. Shoved from behind, Evie had tripped and elbowed Hot Stuff in the gut.

Mortified, she'd crouched to pick up the book he'd dropped. The autobiography of Jonathon Montrose, the man behind Game Plan, no less. Cowboy tech investor, IT savant, Evie's actual hero.

Funny. She'd forgotten that detail. Had that given her the seed of the idea to dare apply for a job with the great man himself? Huh.

Anyway, handing over the book to Hot Stuff, she'd apologised like crazy, while trying not to swoon in his glorious presence, until he'd taken her by both shoulders, strong hands holding her still. He was even bigger up close. And he'd smelled *so* good. When he'd looked down into her eyes, the stormy blue depths of his own holding her in their thrall, she'd forgotten how to breathe until he'd let her go and disappeared into the station with the bustling morning crowd.

Evie let out a soft sigh and glanced his way just as he ran a hand through his overlong dark hair, leaving finger tracks in its wake. All that indolent grace, the sexy stubble and those deeply intelligent-looking eyes—he really added an extra something to the daily commute.

Other commuters came and went, took different trains, adopted random seats, but Hot Stuff always chose the same spot: across the aisle and down three rows from hers. Evie had always been a fan of patterns. It was comforting to know she wasn't the only creature of habit in their little train universe.

"How many apps do you have open at one time?" Zoe fussed, and she swiped them into oblivion. "How does your brain not scramble?"

"It's called multitasking."

Zoe snorted. Then found the Urban Rambler app. Developed by Game Plan, of course. His apps were seriously the best. Evie would be first in line to sign up to Game On—the revolutionary new mobile communication app everyone in the biz was excited about.

Zoe clicked on the *Let's Get Personal* column, flipped the phone so the words were nice and readable and read out loud.

"'*Frankston Line.*' That's us. '*Carriage Three.*' Ditto us. '*To the Bewitching Brunette in the Beauteous Beanies.*'"

Zoe paused a moment for drama before lifting her gaze to Evie's knitted beanie. One of the billion she'd knitted herself. For she really was a fan of patterns.

Today's was silver, with a rainbow pom-pom on top. It didn't *exactly* go with her interview outfit—pea coat over black top and slouchy black pants with fake zips and pockets—all belonging to fashion-plate Zoe, as even computer-nerd Evie wasn't about to turn up to an interview in a Han Solo "I Know" T-shirt, boyfriend jeans and Converse boots—but it did the job.

Zoe said, "Now, hold on to your hat, my friend, because this is going to blow your mind. It says:

*New to your orbit, I find myself struck*
*By your raven locks, your starlit eyes. What luck*
*That I find myself able to see you twice a day.*
*A beacon in a sea of strangers. I must say*
*Your sunshine smiles are my good morning.*
*Your evening sighs my goodnight.*
*If I had the courage I'd say hello.*
*Till then I remain alone in my delight.*
*From Your Appreciative Admirer.*

"Wow," Evie mouthed.

"It's *you*!" Zoe cried. "You are the Bewitching Brunette!"

The schoolboys looked up again, their eyes unglazing this time, enough to give Evie a second glance.

"Well, isn't she?" Zoe asked the boys, waving her hands up and down as if Evie were the prize in a game show. "If this poem wasn't written for you I'll eat your beanie."

Evie tugged off her beanie and shoved it under her butt cheek. Only to have to deal with long strands of dark hair now crackling with static as they stuck to her face.

So, she did have a thing for beanies. She ran naturally cold. Her mum had been the same, needing blankets all through summer. Calling Evie Froglet because of her constantly chilly feet. But it was her granddad who'd taught her how to knit. He'd also taught her how to tie her laces, fix a tractor, cook a perfect steak. To follow her curiosity wherever it might lead her.

Zoe went on. "Lance, for all his good points, is not a romantic man. Telling me my backside looks hot in certain dresses is about as schmaltzy as he gets, bless him. Keeping in mind Lance is a pretty good marker for the average guy, can you see any man on this train who *does* look capable of writing poetry?"

Together they looked. At the scruffy schoolboys now poking wet fingers into one another's ears. The dour gang of goths hanging morosely near the door. The harried working dads with their crooked ties and tired eyes.

As one they turned to the dashing, Byronesque gentleman in the impeccable suit lounging in his seat, reading a book.

Evie swept a hand self-consciously over her hair. It crackled so loudly she quickly put her beanie back on. "Poetry or not, it doesn't matter."

"Why on earth not?"

Evie took her wallet out of her backpack, found a small, crinkled bit of paper and handed it over to Zoe.

"A fortune cookie fortune?" Zoe deadpanned. "From your birthday dinner last week?"

Evie nodded.

"And what does this have to do with Hot Stuff and his undying love for you?"

"Read it."

Zoe did. "'*Bad luck comes in threes. Monkeys, though, they come in trees.*'" After which she burst out laughing. "I...can't...even..."

Evie plucked the piece of paper out of Zoe's

shaking fingers and shoved it into the coin compartment of her wallet. "Ever since I read that stupid fortune things have been weird."

"Weird how?" Zoe asked, wiping her eyes.

"Think."

"Your job!"

"And the sudden losing thereof. The very next day."

"The day after your birthday? You didn't tell me for a week!"

"Because as I stood in the office watching the police take away the computers, you rang to tell me Lance was coming home. You were happy. And rightly so."

Evie knew it was nonsensical, but it felt good to finally be talking about it. Hopefully it would relieve the persistent pressure that had been sitting on her chest since the night of her birthday.

"*Bad luck comes in threes*,'" Zoe said, scratching her chin. "Losing your job was number one."

"Having to move out is number two."

"I told you, you don't have to—"

Evie flapped a *shut up* hand at her friend.

Zoe buttoned her lips. Then promptly unbuttoned them. "There are rules to fortunes, you know. You have to have eaten the entire cookie,

I think. You can't tear the paper. And once you tell someone it no longer comes true!"

"Zoe, it can't 'come true' because it's a computer-generated missive stuck in a random dry cookie." Evie slowly shook her head. "And yet, I feel like it would be remiss of me not to keep an eye out for falling pianos."

Zoe nodded sagely.

Not that Evie was taking it lying down. No, sir. There was the Game Plan interview. One she would never have had the nerve to go for if she hadn't been desperate for work. She was too young, too inexperienced, her only long-term tech job having been for a company who were under investigation for embezzlement and fraud.

Or more specifically Eric—the son of the managing director and her ex-boyfriend—who had pilfered her every last dollar before attempting to flee the country.

Zoe coughed. Then burst into laughter again.

The schoolboys squirmed and sank deeper into their seats, no doubt embarrassed by the loud twenty-somethings in their midst. One perked up enough to realise they were at their stop, and in a rush and flurry they gathered their huge, dirty, dishevelled bags and snaked their way to the doors right as the train lumbered to a halt.

While the carriage emptied and filled, the crowd a seething mass of elbows and wet shoes, of jostling and repositioning, a microcosm of Darwin's survival of the fittest, Evie snuck a glance at Hot Stuff.

He'd glanced up, not at her but at the crowd. He did this every time there was a big shift in people, offering up his seat if he had the chance. Because he was beautiful, well-read *and* a gentleman.

Was it possible—even remotely—*he* had written her a lonely-hearts poem on an app?

The timing fit—morning and evening. The train line too. And there were other hints, clues she couldn't ignore.

*"New to your orbit."* They'd been catching the same train a couple of weeks at most.

*"I find myself struck."* Was that a nod towards the time she'd winded him?

*"Starlit eyes."* She did have an impressive collection of *Star Wars*, *Star Trek*, even *Starman* T-shirts.

She usually went for nice-looking men, with easy smiles and busy mid-level jobs. Men who had no hope of spinning her off course as her mother had been spun. She was only just finding her feet in this town after all. Quietly following her curiosity as her granddad had encouraged her to do.

Hot Stuff was fun to moon over *because* he was out of her league. The thought of him reciprocating—heck, the thought of him even knowing who she was—made her belly turn warm and wobbly.

"Now, hang on a second," said Zoe. "What does this have to do with Hot Stuff and the poem? Ah, I get it. After home and work going up the spout, you don't really think a falling piano is in your future. You believe the logical third spate of bad luck involves your love life. But that's a good thing!"

"In what universe?"

"You can cross messed-up love life off the list. You've already had the *worst* luck there. Eric was a douche. Dumping you. Using you. Framing you—"

"Yep, okay. I hereby concede that point to the prosecution." Evie shook her head. "It doesn't count. He doesn't count. We've been kaput for months. *'Bad luck comes in threes'* means it has to happen after I opened the cookie."

"You've arbitrarily decided a man who looks like Byron's hotter descendant is off-limits because a fortune cookie says it will turn to crap."

Evie looked over at Bryon's hotter descendant. She couldn't help it. Heck, at that very moment the train rounded a bend and a slash of sunlight lit him up like something out of an old film.

"He's dreamy, Evie," said Zoe, though Evie hadn't said a word. "And he wrote you a lonely heart."

Evie blinked, only to find she'd been staring too long as a pair of stormy blue eyes caught on hers. Her breath lodged in her throat. Her cheeks burned as her very blood went haywire.

*Look away,* her subconscious begged. *Look. Away. Now!*

Instead habit overcame instinct, and she smiled.

Growing up in a country town, she'd been smiling at strangers since she'd learned how. Saying hello to anyone who made eye contact. Waving in thanks to cars that stopped to let her cross the street. It was simple good manners.

Now, on a packed train hurtling towards the big city, she felt like an utter fool, her smile frozen into place as those fiercely blue eyes stuck on hers and didn't let up.

Then a small miracle happened. The man blinked, as if coming to from a faraway place. The corner of his mouth kicking north into what could only be a return smile. And then he nodded. Nodded! Sending her a private hello from across the way.

She felt the train concertina as everything beyond the tunnel between their gazes turned fuzzy and out of focus. And then those eyes slid north, pausing at the top of her head. Catching on her beanie, the wool suddenly itching like crazy against her scalp, the bob of the pom-pom like a pulse at the top of her head.

He blinked again, then those stormy eyes slid away.

"Oh, my ever-loving gods," Zoe said. "Did you see that?"

Hell, yeah, she had.

"He couldn't take his eyes off you. Proof he's your Appreciative Admirer!"

Heart kicking against her ribs, Evie let herself follow the possibility of Hot Stuff in the Swanky Suit having a secret crush on *her* to its logical conclusion.

By the look of him he'd eat in fine restaurants, read and understand prize-winning literature, know the actual difference between bottles of wine. From the feel of him when she'd elbowed him then checked him for injury he also wrestled crocodiles, chopped wood for fun and rescued newborn puppies from warehouse fires.

While she lived on cheap cold pizza, spending all weekend in the same holey PJs obliterating strangers gaming online, and she currently slept on an ancient lumpy futon in her best friend's lounge room.

She didn't need a fortune cookie to tell her it would all end in tears.

She looked down at the phone she was spinning over and over in her cold hands.

Her granddad had always insisted her flair for coding was a result of her mum's creative mind. But she'd inherited his practicality too.

Working for Game Plan would be a dream job. Even getting an interview was akin to finding a unicorn in your cornflakes. Especially when no one else would even take her call. She might have been cleared by the feds, but her connection to the embarrassment at her last job made her untouchable.

She couldn't go into that room with thoughts of Hot Stuff filling her head with cotton wool.

Evie glanced up at the electronic readout denoting which stop was next. Real or imagined, the fortune was messing with her head and she had two more stops to put an end to it once and for all.

"You know what I think?" said Evie.

"Rarely."

"If there is even the slightest chance the fortune is real, and I am to be hit with a third blast of bad luck, and it *is* linked to my love life, wouldn't the smart thing be to get it over and done with?"

Zoe grinned. "Only one way to find out."

Which was why, before she had even hatched any kind of plan, Evie pressed herself to her feet and excused herself as she squeezed past the others in her row. Buoyed by Zoe's, "Atta girl!" as she made her way down the carriage.

Armand breathed in deep.

He'd been trying to read a tome on Australian patent law all morning, knowing there was something—some key, some clue—that would unlock the problem he'd been hired to unearth, but the tattooed youth to his left bumped him yet again. He couldn't care less about the piercings and symbols carved into the kid's hair, if only he'd damn well sit still.

Armand willed himself to focus. It was why he'd agreed to uproot himself after all. A challenge, a mystery to sink his teeth into, to deflect his thoughts from hurtling down darker, more twisty paths until it became harder and harder to find his way back.

When the words on the page blurred back at him he gave up. Rubbed his eyes. Looked up.

*People watching,* he had told Jonathon when his oldest friend had asked, expression pained, why he insisted on taking public transport instead of the car and driver he could well afford. A childhood hobby, it had been a useful survival skill once he was an adult.

Armand glanced around the cabin as it rocked gently along the tracks.

There was the Schoolgirl Who Sniffs. Behind her the Man Who Has Not Heard of Deodorant. The Women Who Talked About Everyone They'd Ever Met. The Man Who Carried an Umbrella Even When It Had Not Been Raining.

Now he could add the Boy Who Could Not Sit Still.

A glance out the window showed Armand he was nearing town. Frustrated with his lack of progress, he picked up the book again, opening it just as a shadow poured over the pages.

Armand glanced up, past black jeans tucked into knee-high black boots. Black-painted fingernails on a hand gripping the handle of the backpack slung over a shoulder. Long dark hair pouring over the shoulders of a jacket. Wind-pinked cheeks. And a heavy silver knitted cap with a huge rainbow pom-pom atop, bobbing in time with the swaying of the train.

Fingers lifted off the strap of the bag in a quick wave as the owner of the hat said, "Hi."

"*Bonjour.*"

"You're French?" She glanced sideways, and out of the side of her mouth said, "*Of course he's French.*"

Armand looked past her, but no. She was talking to herself.

When he looked back, she tugged the knitted hat further back on her head and he recognised her as the Girl Who Sang to Herself.

A regular, she often sat deeper back in the carriage with her loud, fair-haired friend. On the days she rode alone she wore big white headphones, mouth moving as she hummed, even giving in to the occasional shoulder wiggle or hand movement.

With her wide, dark eyes and uptilted mouth, she had one of those faces that always smiled, even in repose. Add the headphones and she was practically asking to have her bag stolen. No wonder he'd felt the need to keep an eye on her. He'd seen all too often misfortune descending on those who deserved it least.

When his gaze once more connected with hers it was to find she was watching him still.

"You like to read?" she asked.

Armand blinked. He'd been riding the train for a little over two weeks and it was the first time anyone had tried to strike up a conversation with him. Another reason he'd enjoyed the ride.

"I do."

Her dark gaze slid over his hair, down the arm of his jacket, towards the cover of his book. He turned it over and covered the spine. One didn't become head of an international security firm for nothing.

Armand checked the sign above. With relief he saw his stop was next. She followed his gaze, her mouth twitching before her eyes darted back to his. "How about writing?" she asked, the pace of her words speeding up. "Do you like to write?"

When he didn't leap in with an instant answer, she nibbled on her lip a moment before saying, "I guess there is writing and then there is writing. Texting is wildly different from a thousand-page novel. Or to-do lists compared with…"

As she continued to list the multiple kinds of writing the train slowed and the screech of metal on metal filled his ears, cutting out every other word. The sound dissipating into a hiss as she said, "Or, of course, poetry."

"Poetry?"

She swallowed. Nodded. Her eyes wide. Expectant.

Was he meant to respond in some way? It hadn't felt like a question. In fact, it felt as if he'd stumbled into the middle of someone else's conversation.

And suddenly the singing, the constant smile, the talking to herself, the novelty backpack, his persistent urge to keep an eye on her—it all made sense.

She was a Van Gogh short of a gallery.

He felt his shoulders relax just a little.

"Are you asking if I like poetry?"

She nodded.

"The greats can make you laugh, cry, think, ache, but it depends on the poet. You?"

"I've never really thought about it. I appreciate the skill it must take. Finding words that rhyme. Creating patterns in sound and cadence."

"Look closer. You'll find it's never about a cat who sat on a mat," he said as he pulled himself to his feet.

The woman gripped harder to her backpack strap as she looked up, up, up into his eyes. Her pupils all but disappearing into the edges of her dark irises.

"What is it about?" she asked.

He leaned in a fraction and said, "Wooing."

"Wooing?" she said, her voice a little rough. Her fingers gripping the strap of her bag. "Right. But the thing is, I'm in a transitional period. My life is kind of in upheaval right now. No room for wooing."

"Then my advice would be to stay away from poetry."

The train bumped to a halt, putting an end to the exchange either way. He slid his book into his briefcase.

But she didn't budge an inch.

He angled his chin towards the door. "This is my stop."

"I know." *Blink*. "I mean, right, okay."

She looked as if she had more to say, but the words were locked behind whatever traps and mazes had befallen her afflicted mind.

"*Excusez-moi.*"

A frown flickered over her forehead as the occupants of the carriage swarmed towards the door. Gripping tightly onto the loop hanging from the bar above kept her from smacking bodily against him, but not from stamping down on his foot with the heel of her boot.

He winced, sucking in a sharp breath as pain lanced his toes.

She spun, grabbed him by the arm and said, "Oh, no! Oh, sorry! Sorry, sorry, sorry!"

Then he remembered.

They had spoken once before. His first day on the train she'd elbowed him right in the solar plexus.

If he'd been a man who looked for signs he'd have taken it to mean he'd made a grave error in travelling halfway across the earth in the hopes of being led out of his fugue.

"The Girl with the Perfect Aim," Armand muttered.

"I'm sorry?"

The doors opened, bringing with them a burst of light and chill, rain-scented air. Armand put a hand on the girl's elbow as he squeezed around her, joining the river of people heading out the train doors.

*Strange young woman*, he thought. Yet, he conceded, compelling enough to distract him with alacrity no book or challenge or mystery had yet managed.

He felt those burnished eyes on him long after he'd left the darkness of the station and headed into the grey light of the chilly Melbourne winter's day.

# CHAPTER TWO

EVIE GOT LOST—twice—while trying to find the front door to the Game Plan offices.

For starters, she'd stayed on the train till the next station. No way was she about to follow Hot Stuff in the Swanky Suit. If he'd seen her and was smart—and he certainly appeared to be—he'd have called the police. For oh, how she'd bungled that conversation royally.

Once she'd found the funky, arty little alleyway listed on the Game Plan website, she walked to the end and back without finding the door.

Not her fault. She blamed those stormy blue eyes. That accent. The scent—mysterious, masculine, drinkable. The serious don't-poke-the-bear vibes rippling off the man like a mirage. Wondered if the ten-day stubble sweeping over his hard jaw was rough or soft. How could she make thoughts when he'd held her by the elbow and her nerves had been replaced by fireworks?

Every second of the encounter had been cringe-worthy and it had all been for naught.

Born with a talent for seeing patterns in num-bers, in lines of text, in architecture and nature, Evie did not have the same gift for reading people—a theory backed up by her choice of boyfriends in the past. But she had no doubt Hot Stuff believed her a chip short of a motherboard.

As to whether—or not—he'd written the poem... Who knew?

Stupid fortune cookie. Whether its powers were mystical or merely persuasive, she hadn't been the same since she'd set eyes on it. The sooner she put the whole thing behind her and got on with her life the better.

She stopped in the middle of the alley, looked up into the overcast sky and breathed. "Get it together, kid. And fast."

When she looked back down she found herself in front of a white door tucked into the white brick wall. It had to be the place.

"Okay. You can do this. You want this. You need this."

She'd only just started making a name for herself, working on government contracts, really intricate work. She was most proud of finding and fixing a fissure in the Federal Reserve's security system. One they hadn't even known was there.

But after the way things went downhill in her last job she was tainted by association. Most of her contacts wouldn't take her calls. Those who did wished her luck and got off the phone. Fast.

She had to convince Game Plan to give her a chance by sheer force of personality alone.

Taking a deep breath, she lifted a finger to press the buzzer when the door opened. Of course, they had video surveillance. This was Game Plan. Meaning somewhere some security dude had seen her talking to herself.

Super.

Her heart played a staccato against her ribs as she stepped into a waiting area with white walls, bright fluorescent lighting, potted plants. Needless to say, her jaw dropped an inch when instead of an HR clone an invisible door finally opened to reveal Jonathon Montrose, Mr Game Plan himself.

He looked exactly like he did on the jacket of his autobiography. Rugged. Imposing. Tall. Not as tall as Hot Stuff in the Swanky Suit, mind you.

*Really? You want to go there now?*

*No, I don't!*

*Then focus.*

Evie whipped her beanie off her head, and once more felt the static turn her into a human generator. Madly patting her hair back down, she walked to the man and held out a hand.

"Mr Montrose, I'm Evie Croft. It's an honour. Your *Code of Ethics* textbook is my bible." Evie imagined Zoe holding out both hands, urging her to pace herself.

"From what I hear you can also tear apart code like a demon."

Evie's heart whumped, wondering who he'd heard it from. Her ex-boss? Her ex? The federal police? No way was she getting the job. Nevertheless, she said, "You hear right."

"Shall we?" Montrose held out a hand, ushering her through another door. "Welcome to the Bullpen."

And, while she would have liked to appear even slightly cool, her feet ground to a halt a metre inside the room and she gawped at the sight before her.

Despite the modest entry, the place was gargantuan. Two storeys of glass-walled offices circled the outer rim of the floors above, while the ground floor looked as if it had been hit with a paintball explosion. White walls and floors were splattered with brightly coloured beanbags, cubicles, desks, couches, exercise balls, computers, TVs and in between slouched dozens of guys in jeans, T-shirts and baseball caps, laughing, arguing, creating.

When she found her feet again, Evie followed Montrose along a wall of nooks filled with gaming rooms, VR rigs, darts, pinball machines. One room had rows of bunk beds like a camp dorm.

"When can I move in?"

Montrose laughed. While Evie took it all in—every rivet, every light fitting, every gumball machine, in case she never saw its like again.

Right when Evie felt as if she'd hit sensory overload, Montrose led her up a set of stairs to a huge but relatively subdued office on the second floor, tinted windows looking over the Bullpen below. When he shut the door, everything went quiet.

Evie breathed out in relief when the first woman she'd seen in the place popped her head into Montrose's office and said, "I'm grabbing a coffee. Can I get you guys anything?"

Evie shook her head, frantically gentling her mind. "No, thanks, I'm fine."

"Nothing for me. Thanks, Imogen," said Montrose, and the woman walked back out the door, leaving them alone.

Montrose motioned to a leather tub chair. Evie slid her backpack to the floor and sat.

Montrose sat on the edge of his desk—very much in the power position—crossed his feet at the ankles and began. "Tell me, Evie, why did you leave your last job?"

Evie opened her mouth to give the sensible answer Zoe had forced her to rehearse. Something along the lines of, *After several years of loyal service, I felt I'd achieved all I could and needed a new challenge.*

But she'd always been sensible. Taken small, considered steps. Choosing work she could do with her eyes closed, saving her pennies by sleeping on Zoe's futon. And it had all come crashing down around her ears anyway.

Because luck was out of her hands. Just ask the fortune cookie.

Hang on a second. If losing her last job ticked off the career part of her fortune's portent of "bad luck", this opportunity was uncontaminated. Clean. A fresh start.

And if she truly wanted to make an impression on the likes of Jonathon Montrose, playing it safe wasn't going to work this time.

Forgoing baby steps for a blind leap off a tall cliff, she looked her idol in the eye and jumped.

"You already know why I left, Mr Montrose."

The edge of his mouth twerked. She hoped it was a good sign.

He said, "Indulge me."

Okay then. "I worked for Binary Logistics until my ex-boss's son, Eric—who also happens to be my ex-boyfriend—embezzled from the company. That company is now under investigation by every federal agency there is and, considering my position, my access level, my connection to the guilty party, I was a suspect for co-conspiracy. Thankfully they caught Eric at the airport and he confessed to everything, their forensic decoders followed his trail with ease and I was cleared. But mud like that sticks. Which means you are the only person who has taken my call, much less asked me in for an interview."

She would love to have made it to the end without swallowing but if she didn't wet her dry throat she'd probably pass out.

"And why do you think I would do that?" he asked.

"You're a risk-taker, Mr Montrose. You actually like that I am marginalised. Perhaps I wouldn't have piqued your interest otherwise. You like that it has made me hungry and desperate, because I'll push to prove myself. Qualities you value within yourself."

A muscle flickered at the corner of his mouth. "Maybe. Or maybe I appreciated the gumption it took to even try to get an interview with me, knowing what I know."

Evie's laugh was a little shaky. "Every bit of gumption I have."

From there the interview took a turn into the normal, with Montrose asking about her family—her beloved granddad who'd moved into a retirement village, leaving his farming days behind him—and hobbies—gaming, knitting, hanging with Zoe.

And suddenly it was all over.

Montrose stood and so did she. Grabbing her backpack. And popping her beanie back on her head.

He blinked at the rainbow pom-pom but to his credit said nothing about it. Though he did say, "You are clearly a very bright young woman, Evie. Someone whose name has appeared on my radar more than once. I've heard men with far greater experience gasp over the work you've done, without knowing whose it was."

Evie held her breath.

"Unfortunately, though, I don't have anything for you at this time. I'd suggest you see this career break as an opportunity to look up and out. Read a book, travel, get your hands dirty. In the meantime, we will certainly keep you in mind for future work."

*What? Wait. No. No!*

Evie opened her mouth to state her case. To ask to be given a chance. To drop to her knees and beg if that was what it took. Because, having taken the leap, she could feel the wind in her hair and she wanted more.

But Jonathon was already distracted, and old habits were hard to break. Evie stood, put her beanie back on, grabbed her backpack and—

White noise from downstairs burst into the room as the office door was opened and a voice said, "Do you have a second? I need you to look at…"

The voice came to an abrupt halt.

But it was too late. The accent, the gravel in the tone, the huge amount of air that had been displaced—Evie knew who she'd find when she spun on her heel.

A small noise left her throat as she found herself staring down Hot Stuff in the Swanky Suit. He filled the doorway, the light from below tracing his broad shoulders, his wide stance, his mussed hair.

But gone was the bare hint of that smile he'd given as she'd babbled on about poetry and wooing. The one that had scrambled her brain, making it impossible for her to work out what was real and what wasn't.

Instead his entire body was taut as he glared as if he'd found her in his kitchen boiling his bunny.

"You," Hot Stuff accused, his voice deep and rumbling.

Feeling like a squished bug under the microscope of a stranger's unflattering glare, Evie was finally overcome by the dire reality of her situation and something snapped. "Oh, my God, did you *follow* me here?"

"I believe that is a question I should be asking."

"*Pfft*. Why would I follow *you*?"

The self-assurance in his gaze made her knees go a little weak. And fine, he had a point. But still!

"Excuse me," said Evie. "I made it perfectly clear I'm not interested in your..." She flapped a hand at him, taking in his tousled hair, his arresting face, his slick suit, before blurting, "Your poetry."

Perhaps "perfectly clear" was pushing it, but it had been her intention, which had to count for something.

Yet the man glowered at her, *Why me?* written all over his face.

Seeing him with Montrose's book might have given her the idea to apply for a job with Game Plan. And, come to think of it, had she seen him reading a file with the Game Plan logo on the front? Either way, it didn't seem like admitting it would help her cause in that moment, so she kept her mouth shut.

She saw something move out of the corner of her eye, and was reminded that they weren't alone. She slowly turned to find Jonathon leaning against his desk, looking as if he was enjoying himself immensely.

"I take it you two know one another?" Montrose asked.

Hot Stuff had gone all silent and broody once more, forcing Evie to answer. "We don't know each other, exactly. We catch the same train. Every day. Morning and night. Across the aisle and three rows down."

She took a deep breath in though her nose and caught a scent. Like sailing. And sunshine. Serious masculine heat. Evie knew Hot Stuff had moved to stand next to her. Trying to intimidate her with his presence, no doubt. Arrogant so-and-so.

She half-closed her right eye to block him out as she said, "Though I did elbow him in the gut once. Stood on his foot as well. And that about covers it."

"Is that right?" Jonathon asked, eyes bright.

When Hot Stuff cleared his throat, Evie leapt into the silence with, "Maybe you could do me one favour, Mr Montrose, and say the bit again about how bright you think I am. For I believe your friend has other ideas."

Montrose turned to the man at her side. "Do you?" he asked, laughter lighting his voice. "Do you have other ideas about Evie?"

She glanced sideways to find Hot Stuff gritting his teeth so hard he could pull a muscle.

Deciding to give the guy a tiny break—he had to be as much in shock as she was, after all—she cleared her throat and held out a hand. "I'm Evie, by the way. Evie Croft."

Hot Stuff blinked at her hand, then his gaze lifted to tangle with hers. For a beat. Another. Something dark swirled behind those stormy eyes before he took her hand in his. Of course, it was warm and smooth. The moment they touched a little shock ran up her arm and landed with a sizzle in her chest.

"Armand Debussey," he said in his deep French drawl. Then he took his hand back and looked, deliberately, at Montrose. "What's she doing here?"

scoffed. So much for letting bygones be bygones. "*She* is in the middle of an interview for a coder's dream job," Evie said. Well, it had officially been the end of the interview. Semantics.

"What job might that be?" Hot Stuff asked.

Evie opened her mouth, only to discover she had no idea. She looked at Montrose. And smiled. *Like me! Want me! In a purely professional sense. Okay, stop thinking before you accidentally say any of this out loud.*

Montrose pushed away from his desk and ambled around the edge until he was behind it. Showing who was boss. Then he looked to Armand and said, "She's a forensic code investigator."

Evie bit her bottom lip so hard it hurt. For something in the way he said it made her wonder, made her hope—

"You cannot be serious," said Armand, his voice taut. "She cannot do it. She can't. She's too…" Armand looked at her then, the fire in his eyes filled with danger. And warning.

Evie was a good girl, a smart girl. She kept her goals manageable and took her wins where she could. For her mother had been the exact opposite and it hadn't worked out well for her at all.

But here, now, instead of taking a rational step

back, she felt herself sway towards Armand. Her hands went to her hips, she looked him dead in the eye, and said, "I'm too what?"

The man didn't flinch. If not for his radiating warmth he could have been a statue. The statue said, "You're a dewy-eyed *naïf*, Ms Croft. This place will eat you alive."

As she gawped at him his eyes went to her head. Or, more precisely, her beanie. Then, as if she were three years old, he reached out and tugged on the rainbow pom-pom, no doubt sending it wobbling like crazy.

She smacked his hand away but it was already gone. The man had lightning reflexes. "Well, you, Mr Debussey, are seriously hostile. And what do dewy eyes have to do with my ability to ferret out secret passages, hidden codes, keystones, Easter eggs, back doors in code? With cutting viruses from the flesh of a program without spilling a single drop of blood?"

Armand looked at her as if she was the one talking a foreign language.

"Just because I don't wear fancy suits, or come from a big city, or get my hair to look all perfectly wind-mussed, and finger-fussed, at Ooh-La-La Salon, doesn't mean I'm not killer at what I do. I am the best forensic code investigator you will ever meet, my friend. Put that in your pipe and smoke it."

*Put that in your pipe and smoke it?* Who said that? *Dewy-eyed naïfs, that's who.* As Evie's words swirled around the room like crazy little whirlwinds, she stopped to catch her breath. And wished with all her might she'd never leapt in in the first place. For ever since she'd struggled to regain solid ground.

Biting both lips together now, Evie slowly turned back to Montrose with the full intention of apologising. Only to find something had lit up behind Montrose's eyes. Even with her poor ability to decipher such subtleties, deep inside her instincts shook.

"Right," said Montrose. "Now you've both cleared the air of whatever that was, I'm sure it will make working together all the easier."

"I'm sorry?" said Armand, his voice rich with warning.

"Working together?" Evie asked, her voice sounding as though she were on helium.

"I'm putting you on contract. One project. A trial run, if you will. Congratulations, Evie, the job is yours."

Evie rushed over to the desk and shook Montrose's hand. "Thank you. I won't let you down."

Montrose nodded. "I know you won't. Take a right outside my door and you'll find Imogen's office. She'll get you set up with employee paperwork, security card, pay details etc. Be back here at eight tomorrow."

"Yes, sir. Thank you, sir." Evie spun in a circle—beanie, check, backpack, check—before darting out the door and shutting it behind her. The murmur of rising male voices faded as she hotfooted it to the office next door.

So what if she'd be working in the same building as Armand Debussey? And hadn't asked about pay, benefits, hours? She had a job! And not just any job! Forensic code investigation for Game Plan!

Her luck had surely turned.

She'd just have to steer clear of Armand Debussey as much as humanly possible, which shouldn't be hard in a company this size. And over time, her discomfort around him would fade.

And she'd remember this day not as one of her most bumbling but as one of her best.

Frustration riding every inch of him, Armand stalked behind Jonathon's desk, opened the minibar and pulled out a bottle of Scotch. He didn't bother asking Jonathon if he wanted one. He could get his own damn drink.

Armand poured himself just enough to cover the bottom of the glass, needing the burn in his throat to take the edge off whatever had just yanked him so vehemently from the mouth of *ennui*. Had made him burn.

He glanced at the screen embedded in Jonathon's desk to see the note Jonathon sent to Imogen about Evie Croft. A contract, as promised. One project. Armand translated Australian dollars to Euros and scowled at the pay offer. Why anyone chose to work for the man he had no idea.

"It's not even ten in the morning," Jonathon noted.

Armand tossed back the drink, wincing at the heat. "It's midnight in Paris."

"Then go for your life. And to answer your burning question," said Jonathon, "she did not follow you here, she applied for the job a few days ago. Nice girl. Next-level intelligence. Yet I had decided not to hire her when you came storming in."

"What the hell changed?"

"You tell me."

Armand knew Jonathon was baiting him. And why. Armand took a long, deep breath and waited. He could wait for ever, if that was what it took. One good thing about not giving a damn—his indifference knew no bounds.

Jonathon squinted his way. "Is it hard for you to believe I hired her on her merits? Is it because she's a woman?"

"*Non*," Armand scoffed, wounded by the accusation. "*Mon Dieu*—"

"English, please."

"No."

"Is it because she's young?" Jonathon asked. "How old is she?"

"I didn't ask. We're not allowed to these days." Armand looked to the ceiling and muttered.

"*En Anglais, s'il vous plaît*," said Jonathon.

"You understood every word."

Jonathon grinned. "Mid-twenties, I'd say. The age of blissful ignorance and creative hubris. An advantage in her line of work. While you, five years older at most, bear the weight of the entire world on your well-bred shoulders."

Not any more, Armand thought, tipping the last drop of Scotch onto his tongue before putting the glass on the desk.

"How did it come about on your daily train trips, morning and night, across the aisle and three rows down, you came to think her not clever?"

Armand merely slanted him a look.

"Save it for another time, then. Until then I assure you—Evie Croft is special."

Armand railed against the thought as the embers inside him flared. But he listened, as the mountain of paperwork—legal documents, in-house communications, news articles, company reports—Jonathon had foisted on him had not yet yielded results.

Jonathon went on. "One of my guys picked up on her chatter online a couple of years back. Tough talk about cracking one of our most complicated games. Turned out it wasn't just talk. The last company she worked for was a lumbering dinosaur, a house of cards waiting to tumble, but her work therein was inspired. I'd go so far as saying she's a prodigy."

Armand ran a hand down his face. He knew that look in Jonathon's eye. The gleam. For Jonathon was no longer pulling his leg.

"If it's not because she's a woman," said Jonathon, "and it's not because she's young, and now you know she can do the work, do we still have a problem here?"

Armand wanted to say *no problem*. To accept

the inevitable. For all he wanted was to fix Jonathon's problem and go home. Back to the familiar, the safe. But for some reason he couldn't say the words.

"It's the dewy-eyed *naïf* thing, isn't it?"

Armand dropped his face into his palm and laughed, the sound hollow, humourless. "I knew that would come back to haunt me."

"I'd go as far as to say that's exactly why Ms Croft got under your skin just now. You are worried when you bump into her in the hall she might spark some proof of life within you. You didn't die that day, my friend, no matter how it might sometimes feel you did..."

Armand shook his head. Just once. But it was enough. Enough for his old friend to know he'd hit the edge of that which Armand would accept.

"What are we to do?" Jonathon asked. "I will not launch my very expensive, very important program until you assure me it is safe. If you believe you don't need Ms Croft and her special skills in order to make that happen then I'll tell Imogen to send her home right now. It's completely up to you."

With his high-level contacts, hands-on experience tracking the worst kinds of men, even his very name, Armand could chase down public information and private conversations, money and mayhem, promises made in huts and boardrooms. He had blown open drug deals, illegal gun sales, fraud rings and worse. He could speak five languages and understand many more.

But when it came to the inner workings of computer code, he was at a loss.

And yet Armand's nostrils flared as he fought against the overwhelming need to make the call that meant not having to deal with the likes of Evie Croft. Those big dark eyes that hid nothing of what she felt. The tip-tilted mouth with the full bottom lip she nibbled on more than could possibly be necessary. That constant frisson of energy that crackled around her. Those odd knitted hats. The woman was a magnet for trouble.

Armand breathed deep, only to find himself enveloped in a lingering cloud of feminine perfume. Or perhaps it was shampoo. It smelled like cherries, of all things.

The women of his experience wore designer scents. They did not smell like *fruit*. Or wear pom-poms on their headwear. Or have cartoon characters printed on their backpacks. They did not have backpacks at all.

He pictured Evie Croft leaning towards him, hands on hips, lips pressed together, dark eyes flashing, making fun of his suits, his haircut. All while in the midst of a job interview.

She might be dangerously naïve, she might even be a bit of a head case, but she had fortitude. He had to give her that.

Then, before he saw it coming, her image was replaced with another—little black dresses, diamonds and pearls, pale blue eyes filled with judgement, the swing of a neat blonde ponytail heading out the door.

Armand wiped a hand down his face.

At least he could be sure Jonathon had it wrong on one score—Evie Croft was as far from his type as it was possible to be.

"Give her a shot," Armand said. Hearing the rawness of his voice, he took a moment to swallow. "But she is on trial."

"Why do you think I put her on contract? Now go forth. Find out why my perfect program is glitching so that I can launch the damn thing. Knowing nothing that happens between you and Ms Croft will concern HR."

Armand opened his mouth to vehemently deny the accusation.

"Read my lips," said Jonathon. "I Do Not Care. Now that's settled, why did you come storming in? You wanted me to look at something."

Armand searched back through the quagmire of the past ten minutes for the answer then remembered the piece of paper. He found it scrunched up on the floor near his feet. He pressed it open, saw the lines of code he'd hoped Jonathon could explain to him, before folding it neatly and putting it back in his pocket.

Jonathon laughed. "Something for your new workmate to sort out tomorrow, then?"

"So it would seem." Armand pulled himself out of the chair and ambled to the door, pausing with his hand on the frame. "You know what made that whole debacle worth it?"

"I can't wait to hear."

"'*Yes, sir. Thank you, sir.*'"

Jonathon's face fell to his desk, landing with a thud. "I felt like a dinosaur."

"Serves you right. Sir."

Armand shut the door behind him with a soft click and moved to the railing to look out over that which the staff called the Bullpen.

He took a step back when he saw a rainbow-coloured pom-pom bobbing through the space.

Used as he was to working with serious men—men who in another era would be warriors and guerrillas and pirates and Vikings, men with scars covering every inch of their bodies, inside and out—working around the kids down below in their running shoes and cheap deodorant had been a stretch.

And now he'd been lumbered with the Girl Who Sang to Herself.

He told himself he did not find her whimsy charming. That it was to her detriment. But the truth was he hadn't only kept an eye on her to make sure no one robbed her blind while she listened to music with her eyes closed.

The moment he first set eyes on her he'd not been able to look away. The way she smiled, the way she laughed—she had surely been lit from within. Making the train trips home in the chill Melbourne evenings feel not so dark at a time when he'd thought he'd never feel warm again.

When a man had lived with ice in his veins as long as Armand had, warmth was not a relief. As his sluggish blood heated, straining to pulse faster through his stiff, cold arteries, every part of him ached.

Now she'd be here, every day, till he got the job done.

He wasn't sure how to bear it.

Worse, he wasn't sure he had it in him any more to try.

# CHAPTER THREE

EVIE USUALLY LOVED the train ride into the city.

The rocking of the carriage, the soft *chooga-chooga* of the train rumbling over the tracks, the pockets of suburbia swishing by.

Unable to bring such sensitive work home, she'd had no choice but to chat, listen to music and let her mind wander, riding those blissful streams of creative consciousness that only come with doing nothing. To daydream.

On her own today—as Zoe had been picked up early to take a plane to Sydney for a meeting with the head designers at her work—Evie was a bundle of nerves, counting the stops till one Armand Debussey was due to hop on.

Instead of staring at the train doors all the way into town she worked on her latest beanie.

Her mother had died when she was six, so Evie's granddad had raised her. An old-school gent with a quick mind and flashes of accidental feminism, he'd taught her how to tie her shoelaces, how to fix a tractor, and how to knit.

Right now all she had was a square of yellow, but in the end it would have ear flaps with plaits on the end that could be tied under the chin. Granddad's request for a woman named Corinne who'd just moved into his retirement village on the outskirts of her home town.

But her mind was so scattered, she had to unravel a row and start over three times.

Giving up, she took out her phone and scrolled despondently through the real-estate app until she found three share houses that didn't seem too awful to contemplate.

She called the first to find it already taken.

She called the second. The phone rang out.

She called the third. The ring tone buzzed in her ear as the train doors opened. It was Armand's stop.

For a moment Evie thought he might not appear. He could have taken a different train. Hopped on a different carriage—

"Hello? Hello?" a chipper female voice called in her ear.

"Oh, hello," Evie said into her phone. "Hi. My name's Evie and I'm calling about the share room."

"Super. Well, the fee listed is weekly. The place is freshly painted. Bed supplied, but BYO linen. The room is a double. Has a view of the park."

Evie sat taller as the voice continued extolling the virtues of what sounded like the perfect set-up.

But then her brain hit *pause* as a familiar dark form punched a hole in the sunny doorway. All sexy mussed hair and beastly countenance, the form lingered a beat before moving into the carriage, the fluorescent lights playing over the hard angles of his unfairly beautiful face.

In the back of her mind Evie heard, "Halvesies on Wi-Fi, electrics and water. Walk to train, shops and bars."

Armand's unerring gaze had found hers, with that potent mix of stormy blue and a French sense of not giving a hoot. And the voice faded to a distant whir.

Evie braced herself for a nod hello before he would no doubt take his usual seat. She could then spend the next ten minutes ignoring him before they got off at the same stop. Then she'd pause to tie her non-existent laces before walking in the same direction but not with him—

Wait. Oh, no. He was coming her way.

Evie's knitting slipped on her lap and the last three casts slid from the needle. Muttering under her breath, she quickly swaddled the mass of yellow wool, one-handed, and shoved it into her backpack.

"Is your friend not here?"

*Good morning to you too*, Evie thought as she looked up. Only when her eyes met his—to find him staring blankly at the greenery on top of her pumpkin-shaped beanie—did it hit her that he knew she usually sat with a friend.

Meaning he *had* noticed her too. And paid attention.

"*New to your orbit, I find myself struck/By your raven locks, your starlit eyes. What luck...*" The accent reciting the poem in her head was very definitely French and she shook her head hard to make it go away.

Armand took it as an answer. Pointing at the spare seat across from her, he asked, "May I?"

Evie swallowed. "All yours."

"Sorry?" said the voice in her ear.

"Sorry," Evie parroted back. "Sorry, you dropped out for a second. I'm on the train."

Evie crossed her legs as Armand took a seat, tugging on her ruffled skirt, which hadn't seemed short when she'd put it on that morning. Her high brown boots with the even longer socks were no protection, as his legs were so long her bare knees rested in between his.

Not that he seemed to notice. As usual he had a book in his hand and simply got on with reading. Beauty and brains. It was seriously hard not to sigh.

And then the train took off, rocking Evie's legs into Armand's, the shift of his suit pants rubbing roughly against the bare skin of her knees. This was going to be the longest ride of her life.

"Though the rats are gluten-free," said the chipper voice in her ear. "Dairy intolerant and the smell of fruit makes them gag. Any housemate must respect that."

"I'm sorry, did you say rats?"

Armand looked up, frowning. It was his default face. Evie pointed at her phone. He nodded and went back to his book.

After a pause, the voice in her ear said, "Yes."

"You have pet rats?"

The voice scoffed. "I am no more their master than they are mine."

Evie bit her lip and thought about the supplied bed, the walk to the train, the view of a park. "How many rats?"

"I couldn't say. Their numbers ebb and flow. Though Rowena is pregnant right now so a swell is imminent."

Scrunching her eyes tight, Evie said, "Okay, well, thanks. I'll get back to you." And then she hung up.

When she opened her eyes it was to find Armand watching her. The frown was still in place, but it seemed to have softened. Just a little.

Evie waved her phone at him. "Looking for a new place to live."

"With rats?"

"I'm hoping they'll be optional."

"A new job and a new home," he noted.

"You could say I'm in a transitional period."

"Yes, you mentioned that. Yesterday on the train."

"Did I? Well. Any chance we could forget that entire conversation?"

"Already done."

"Super." She smiled, then bit down on her lip.

His gaze dropped to her mouth and a crease formed above his nose. His eyes darkened, as if a cloud had passed over the sun, then he looked away and out the window. Conversation over.

Evie rolled her eyes at herself. Get a grip! Then the train tilted as it rocketed around a corner and Evie's knee slammed into Armand's, before sliding a good inch or two up his leg.

Evie grabbed her seat and shuffled back as deep as she could. While Armand's only reaction was the slide of his gaze to the point of impact.

Did it not bother him the way it bothered her?

Or did he not move because he liked it? Could it be, despite evidence to the contrary, he had a little crush on her too? Had he in fact written a poem about her? To her? For her?

There was one way to find out—she could just ask. *Hey, Armand, did you write me a love poem and publish it on Urban Rambler's lonely-hearts page?*

But if it was a no she'd not only have to see him on the train, but at work as well. And mixing personal life and work life was a recipe for disaster. She'd learned that lesson the hard way.

And what about the slim chance he'd say *yes*?

She came over a little wobbly in the belly, tingly behind the knees. Which was more than enough of a reason for a case of don't ask, don't tell.

Needing to say something lest she say the one thing she could not, she said, "No Australian patent-law book today?"

A few moments went by before Armand looked up. He lifted the cover of his book—this one by a certain Nathaniel Hawthorne.

"Any good?"

Armand surprised her by asking, "You haven't read it?"

"Might have seen the movie."

Armand's sigh was long-suffering.

"Don't panic. I do read. I'm in my granddad's retirement-village book club. This month we're reading a JD Robb. Futuristic cop romance. They're awesome."

Armand's face remained impassive. But Evie swore she saw a flash of sufferance behind his eyes. The guy had no idea what he was missing. "And when you're not reading?"

"I game."

Armand winced. This time it was obvious even to her, the queen of misreading people.

"Don't knock it till you try it. The good games, the really great ones—it's not about the effects, or the amazing CGI, it's about the story. Those ones get under your skin, make you think. Make you laugh, cry, even sigh."

She realised all too late she'd mirrored his words from the day before when he'd spoken of great poetry.

Maybe it was best to get it out there, to be sure. Otherwise the energy used to keep a lid on it might cause her to implode.

She sat forward, her hands draping over her knees. "Armand. Can I call you Armand? Of course I can; it's your name."

His gaze remained on hers, his eyes so dark she could not make out the colour at all.

"About yesterday, on the train, when I asked if you like poetry…"

He sat forward too. He smelled amazing. Clean, laundered. Edible. "Didn't we already agree it was forgotten?"

"Mmm-hmm."

A sunbeam chose that moment to hit the window of the train, sending shards of diffused light over his face. The man looked like a prince. One who had left the palace long ago, heading off on a thankless crusade to slay a dragon or rescue a princess or free a kingdom. Only he'd got lost along the way—head injury? Magic spell?—and couldn't reconcile how he found himself on a train heading towards inner-city Melbourne.

"Ms Croft," he said, "Jonathon does not hire lightly. He does so with recklessness, at times, but always in the hope of creating magic. You have been given a chance to be a part of something important. Make it count."

The train lurched and her fingers grazed his knee. She jerked them back.

Then he was standing, moving through the crowd, and she realised the train had reached their stop.

Evie grabbed her bag, apologised as she

squeezed past legs, stepped over bags. Once outside the train she caught up to Armand.

He turned quickly, and she nearly banged into him.

"I have a stop to make first," he said.

She took another step back. "Right. Okay. Well, I might see you around work."

He looked at her in that long, slow, considering way he had, then with a nod he slipped through the crowd and was gone.

Reading normal people was hard enough. Reading a man who acted like Yoda had had a makeover and ended up on the cover of *GQ* was impossible.

Leaving Evie to lift her arms in a shrug of utter confusion.

But nobody paid her any heed.

She shifted her backpack into a more comfortable position and headed off to the first day of the rest of her life.

Having used her shiny new security key to enter the Game Plan building, Evie walked into the Bullpen. The colour, the noise, the light like an elixir to her soul.

Armand had hit on something. She'd been given a second chance here. A chance to do things differently this time. It might even be time to forgo the baby steps for bigger strides. For third chances were rare.

So, rather than hiding herself away, she introduced herself to anyone who looked up from their work, determined not to take cover from office politics. Anything to make sure she wasn't blindsided like last time.

"You're Evie Croft, right?" asked a guy about her age.

"Um, yes."

"Your arrival was pinged in the daily company email alongside a Roger and a Phil. Pretty easy guess. You might not have noticed but this place is testosterone-heavy."

By the looks of the room, the testosterone levels were pretty mild, but she just smiled and shrugged. "Used to it."

"I'm Jamie."

Evie shook his hand. Felt the familiar rough thumb pads of a guy who gamed. Caught the gleam of interest in his eyes and let go.

Fortune cookie or no fortune cookie, she was going to make good decisions, the first of which was to keep work and monkey business a million miles apart.

"I'd better get started," she said, backing away. "Nice to meet you."

"See you around, Evie."

Evie followed the instructions Imogen had given her the day before, heading back up the stairs that led to Jonathon's office, before heading down a dark hall with a single door at the very end. No glass here. Very mysterious.

She went to open the door to find it locked. Now what?

Then she noticed a small discreet pad lodged into the wall, with buttons the same colour as the paint. A keycode? Fingerprint? She tried hers but nothing happened.

She turned, thinking to head…somewhere, when the door opened inward with a flourish.

Evie jumped back as a dark figure appeared in the doorway, backlit by a dim glow. "Jeez, you scared me!"

"Apologies."

That voice… "Armand?"

Without another word, he pressed the door open wider and motioned for her to come inside. A golden glow created a halo around his profile—strong nose, sombre forehead, unkempt hair shading his stormy blue eyes.

"I'm really not following you, I promise."

He opened the door a fraction wider, giving her a glimpse of dark wood and low lamplight, a pair of small lounge chairs—elegant dark brown to match the rest of the room. Coffee table, ditto. Bookshelves. It was like something out of a gothic novel. It suited him to a T.

She kept her feet firmly planted in the hall.

"Are you waiting for a formal invitation, Ms Croft?"

"To what? Here?" She poked her head inside, and counted the desks—one, two. "With you? I'm to be working in here with you?"

"For me," he qualified.

Well, that was way better.

"Of course, if you are second-guessing your decision to take on the role, I can let Jonathon know—"

"Are you kidding? I'm delighted. Thrilled! Look at me." She stretched a huge smile across her face to prove it. Then, hitching her backpack higher onto her shoulder, she nudged past, catching a waft of lemongrass, of cedar, of clean, groomed man.

Evie took off her beanie and blew out a breath, a wave of hair sweeping away from her face. "Any chance you might have told me this morning?"

The edge of Armand's mouth flickered, before

his face settled into its usual blank cool. One hand slid into the pocket of his suit pants, his scruffy hair slipping over one eye. "The work is sensitive. We will not be discussing such things in public venues."

She opened her mouth to say *Won't we, now?* but, considering the kind of work she was used to doing, she believed him.

When Evie turned Armand had moved deeper into the room. She tipped back so fast she had to take a step away. "Look, you were right. This morning in the train. Today is a new beginning for me. As such I'd like for us to start again too." She held out a hand. "Hi, I'm Evie Croft. Nice to meet you."

The pools of golden light created shadows upon shadows over his dark form, so she nearly missed the spark that flickered to life in his eyes before he reached out and took her hand in his.

Once again, a zap of electricity shot from his hand through hers like a delicious little shock.

"Armand Debussey," he drawled. *"Enchanté."*

She offered a most professional nod, then quickly pulled her hand away. "So, what now?"

Armand glanced at her a beat longer before his dark gaze swept past her and he motioned with a tilt of his chin. "Now we get to work."

She moved to follow the direction of his gaze, but at the last moment saw him surreptitiously rub his thumb into the palm, as if trying to rid himself of pins and needles.

Had he felt it too? The zap? No. Surely not. It was probably just nerves. Or static electricity from the commercial carpet.

A small voice in the back of her head said, *Work, monkey business, a million miles apart.* Her train crush and his poem—or not—could not matter from this moment on. They were colleagues, nothing more. Zip. The end.

One of the desks had a single yellow banker's lamp, paper calendar, a pristine notebook, pencils lined up just so. Definitely his.

In the other corner, the second desk was big, shiny and black. Hinged for sitting or standing. Ergonomic chair. Linked to three huge monitors. And was that...? It was! An encrypted solid-state hard drive, the likes of which she'd only heard rumoured.

"Please tell me that's mine."

"It's certainly not mine."

That was all she needed to hear.

She all but ran across the room, dumping her backpack, gaze dancing from one glorious technological wonder to the next. Whatever she had been hired to do, she'd been given state-of-the-art hardware with which to do it.

She'd set up employee name, password, fingerprint and retinal ID with Imogen the day before. With a single swipe of her finger, the system turned on.

"Pinch me," she muttered.

*"Pardon?"* Armand said, now leaning back against the edge of his desk, hands gripped lightly around the wood, watching her settle in.

Her heart fluttered like a butterfly at the sight. But she pushed the feeling back down.

"Okay, then, boss. Where do I begin?"

Armand did the chin-tilt thing, motioning to a note on her desk. Apparently, she was to click on the only icon on the screen and follow the prompts.

She'd been so untethered by the events of her past week she couldn't wait to get her teeth stuck into something solid.

As for Hot Stuff in the Swanky Suit? She'd find a way to work with him without swooning, or snapping, or she'd die trying.

Armand, who wished to get back to the slew of work he had to get through, instead watched as

Evie brought a flexible plastic rectangle out of her backpack, uncurled a thin cord from one corner and plugged it into the hard drive of the main computer.

He might not know much about software, but he had a handle on mechanics. And this was not regulation. "May I ask what it is you think you are doing?"

"Hmm?"

He pointed to the foreign object on her desk.

"Cool, right? Not a Qwerty keyboard. Programmed so that only I know the order of the keys."

Armand, who typed with two fingers and only when forced, asked, "Why?"

"Security."

"I'm not sure Jonathon would concur—"

"He knows. I emailed him the specs last night."

"Again, why?"

Evie's fingers stretched as they hovered over the shiny black contraption. "Fair question, since I'll be working with...sorry, *for* you. In my last job, someone used my access code to embezzle from the company."

The hairs rose on the back of Armand's neck

and his fingers curled in on themselves as he glanced in the direction of his friend's office.

"It's okay," Evie said. "Jonathon knows."

Armand glanced back at her and stretched out his hands. It wasn't okay. It wasn't even close to being okay.

"How did it happen?"

"The person, the embezzler, was the boss's son. And my ex-boyfriend. Turned out he'd hidden cameras in my office so he could copy my key strokes."

She rested her hands gently over her blank keyboard then blinked at him, her eyes big, shining, sombre. "I was a total dewy-eyed *naïf.* The only reason I don't still lie awake at night berating myself is that the authorities are confident the money will all be recovered."

She'd been worse than naïve. As Armand saw it, she'd been grossly negligent. But he also knew about lying awake at night, riddled with regret.

"If he'd been smart enough to code, if he'd even touched my computer I'd have known it. I could have stopped him. Ironically it was the fact he was clueless that gave him the advantage over me."

Armand bristled. He had degrees in law, economics and art history. He owned an internationally renowned private-security company. He could defuse a bomb with his bare hands. But if a computer locked up he'd have to call Tech Support.

Not that he'd been near a bomb in some time. Now he spent his days sorting fake Picassos from real for his family's art collections, his mother claiming the genteel world of art was where someone with his intellect ought to be. Not out "playing the hero", nearly killing them all with worry.

"Anyway," Evie went on, "it taught me to be extra-vigilant. No one's ever going to pull the wool over my eyes again. If you'd like I can show you how this thing works…"

Armand held up both hands. But it was shiny and space-age and he was a man. Curious despite himself, he asked, "Where did you find such a thing?"

"It's a prototype. I invented it."

"You?"

She nodded slowly. "Yeah, me. Ironically if I'd not worked all those extra hours at my last job, I'd have had more spare time to finish this baby and Eric would never have had the chance to do what he did. Anyway, while I can only hope you don't plan to frame me for embezzlement, I'm using the keyboard and that's that."

Armand waved a hand in acquiescence. "Have it."

Which she did.

Leaving Armand to wonder what the hell Jonathon was thinking.

Perhaps she was innocent, but she'd been duped. Her instincts were less than exemplary. Her relative youth might be an asset when it came to the job at hand, but her naivety was a proven liability. She jeopardised the entire team.

Armand sat behind his desk, running a hand over the bristles on his chin. He knew exactly what Jonathon was thinking. The hero complex that terrified his parents would have him fall head over heels for one ingenuous brunette.

Jonathon had been a player his whole life. Gambling with ideas, with investment and invention. Only this time he was playing with people.

One who wanted this job with her whole heart.

One who had no heart left.

Meaning the sooner the job was done, the sooner he could leave the game. Go back to Paris. And sink back into a life of ease and comfort where he'd never put a loved one in the path of danger again.

* * *

Two hours later Evie's leg ached from jiggling.

The icon on the smaller screen had led to a slew of training videos covering everything from how to turn on a computer to proper workplace language, each finishing with twenty-five inane multiple questions to answer at the end. It was mind-numbing. Life-sapping.

She glanced up to find Armand still poring over the papers on his desk. The man's focus was impressive. Figuring he could keep it up for hours, she wriggled on her seat, and with a few relatively easy clicks found her way into the back end of the program she'd been forced to undergo. Another half an hour and she was done. Each program now registered as complete.

"Done!" she called out.

Armand took a moment to glance up at the analogue clock on the wall beside his desk. "You're finished?"

"Yep. What's next? Unless I've been put in this room with you as some kind of scientific experiment. See how long it takes me to crack. Or you!"

Armand slowly leant back in his chair. "Am I to expect this level of chatter to continue?"

"Oh, yeah. My granddad was a big one for curiosity. Whether I was keen to know about tractor engines, or constellations, or ant hills, or bones in the wrist, he'd take time to answer any questions I posed. I posed a lot."

Ah, Granddad. Evie wondered what he was doing in that moment. He seemed to truly be enjoying life in the lovely local retirement village, which was so wonderful. Costing her every spare penny to cover the rental, but better that than sell the farm—his lifeblood, her home.

She blinked back to the present to find Armand sitting still, breathing slowly, exuding such an air of rakish sophistication he could well have been part-vampire. She'd always had a thing for vampires.

"My turn," Evie trilled. "If I'm Chatty Cathy, why are you taciturn?"

He blinked. For him that was as telling as a flinch. "I don't see the point in speaking unless one has something of worth to say."

"Ouch. That was a dig at me, right?"

The edge of his mouth flickered and Evie held her breath. A smile? Was it coming? But no, his face eased back into its usual watchful repose.

"Here's something worth discussing," said Evie. "Tell me about the project I'll be working on."

Armand blanked, and sat up tall. "We'll get to that. Why don't you take a break?"

Evie rolled her eyes and stood, grabbing her backpack and heading for the door. But she stopped before she made it past his desk. "You will have to tell me eventually, you know. Give me full and proper access to all the boxes with the wires and engines and microchips."

She paused, deciding how best to put a dent in her cohort's perfect façade. "It's not a big leap to figure out what I'll be doing. I'm a hacker. Jonathon needs me to hack. Find errors and to clean up the mess. Right?"

Anything? A glimmer of surprise? Of admiration at her powers of deduction? Nope. *Nada.*

"Here's something to mull over—while I have yet to find a system, a program, a game, a brand of software that I cannot infiltrate, I can't analyse that code unless I actually see the code."

Armand rose, forcing Evie's chin to tilt as she looked up into his shadowed face. Only he moved to the shelves, where he picked out a heavy-looking text and brought it back to his desk, where once again he sat.

Evie felt totally flustered. Not that there was anything rushed about him—more an overwhelming sense of power well-leashed.

He picked up a pencil, perfectly sharpened, and

gripped it between his teeth as he sat back in his chair and began to read.

Which was when it hit her. "Where's your computer, Armand? Your cell phone? I see pencils, I see notebooks, I see a lot of paper. You're a technophobe!"

She clapped her hands together before jumping out into a star. *Ta-da!* Only her audience wasn't clapping. She shuffled her feet back together. "I'm going on a break now. Want anything? Coffee? Tea?"

She—very smartly—stopped herself from saying *Me?* Even in jest. She hadn't needed to take a quiz on Appropriate Interpersonal Office Relations to know it was best to steer clear of those kinds of conversations with Armand from now on.

"No? Then I'll see you in half an hour."

Evie headed down the stairs, grabbed an apple from her bag and made her way towards the exit in search of fresh air. Though she soon found herself waylaid by the noise and bling of the Bullpen.

She slowed, dawdling past the little alcoves to find a couple of guys duelling on pinball machines, a couple talking string theory while playing vintage Ataris, and—

"Evie."

Evie spun on her heel. "Jamie. Hi."

"Looking for someone?"

"Break time," she said, holding up her apple.

He blinked as if he'd never seen such a strange food. "I'm thinking you've not yet found the Yum Lounge."

"I have not."

Jamie cocked his head, motioning for her to follow. Follow she did, but not before glancing up the stairs as if expecting to see Armand hiding in the shadows, watching over her like her own personal avenging angel.

The "Yum Lounge" turned out to be Game Plan's private restaurant. Jamie pointed the way to a two-seater table together in the corner of the room. When their meals came out they looked and tasted like something out of *Masterchef.*

Evie sat back, holding a hand over her belly. "Amazing. But I do not want to ask what that just cost me."

"Not a cent," said Jamie with a grin.

She sat up straight. *Oh, no. No, no, no.* "No, Jamie, you can't… This wasn't…"

He grinned. "Relax. I didn't. It's all part of the package."

"Seriously? Pinch me." Evie held out her arm.

Jamie grinned at her. Then reached out and gave her arm a pinch. Right as a shadow fell over the table.

As one they looked up to find Armand looming over them. Hands in his pockets, face dark and stormy.

Cheeks heating like crazy, Evie tugged her arm back to check her watch. She'd been gone for thirty-five minutes. Dammit.

"Back to the grindstone," she said, quickly wiping her mouth with a napkin and pushing back her chair.

"Stay," Armand commanded.

Evie made a point of sitting upright like a good girl.

Something flickered behind Armand's dark eyes before he added, "I am not your keeper, Ms Croft. You were not answering your phone, therefore I sought you out to let you know I will not be in the office when you return."

"Oh. Okay." Glancing at Jamie, who was watching them carefully, she was judicious in her choice of words. "This morning, the keypad..."

"Programmed."

"And what should I work on while you're gone?"

"I've left a note."

"Cool. Great!" she effused, his soberness somehow making her want to double up on the sunshine factor. "I'll get on it right away."

As if he knew exactly what she was doing, Armand drawled, "Enjoy your lunch, Ms Croft," before walking away.

"I did thanks," she called. Then after a pause added, "Mr Debussey."

His next step may have faltered slightly. He was too far away to truly tell.

"Wow," said Jamie, drawing out the word. "Wait a minute—you're working with *him*?"

"I am."

"Huh. He's been lurking around here for a few weeks, holed up in Jonathon's office. Very cloak and dagger. In fact, there's a pool going. Is he an auditor? A psychic? Private eye? I have fifty bucks on bodyguard."

Despite not enjoying Armand's clear hesitation in giving up the details to her, she had to figure he had good reason. With a friendly shrug she went with, "First day—still not quite sure."

Jamie squinted, but took her word for it. "Is he as big a stiff as he seems?"

Evie opened her mouth before snapping it shut as a strange kind of protectionist sensibility washed over her.

Armand might be difficult, but she had to trust that Jonathon Montrose had put them together for a reason. And, well, something about him made her feel as though he was used to looking out for other people rather than the other way around.

"First day, remember," she said.

"Right."

Evie glanced through the restaurant in the direction Armand had gone. She could practically see the trail of his mysterious aura. Wondered what stories, what secrets lurked beneath the elegant façade. Such as...had he ever written a lonely heart?

"Jamie?"

"Yes, Evie?"

"Have you ever written poetry?"

"Poetry? Good God, no. Unless...would you like me to?"

Her gaze slammed back to his. "What? No! I didn't mean it that way. It was just a random query..." She shook her head and pressed herself to standing. "Anyway, I'd better get back to work. I'll see you round."

Jamie opened his mouth as if he had more to add, but she spun on her heel and bolted.

# CHAPTER FOUR

ARMAND KNOCKED ONCE before striding into Jonathon's office.

Imogen looked up from where she was taking notes. Without a word she unfolded herself from the chair and melted from the room. Why couldn't Evie be more like her? Dignified, mindful, not disturbing in any way?

Jonathon checked the contraption on his wrist where a watch ought to be. "A little over three hours till you stormed into my office. My money was on one. How goes it?"

"Interminably."

"You don't say."

"She can't sit still. She's always shifting position. Twirling, stretching, rocking back and forth."

Armand had had a kid in his first platoon with an attention-deficit condition. A good kid— super-fit, keen, but a total daydreamer. Armand was sure he'd lost years off his life trying to keep the kid alive. Until the day the kid's number was up.

He ran a hand down his face. Not going there. Not any more.

"Are you punishing me for something? Did I bruise your delicate feelings in some way?"

"When will you realise Evie Croft is not penance, she's a gift. Learn from her. Guide her. Find common ground. Find a way to work together. You'll thank me."

Armand slouched into the chair across from Jonathon's desk. "She's on to me."

"She's into you?"

"*On to*," Armand enunciated, certain Jonathon had heard him just fine. "She called me out for not having a computer."

"Armand, old friend, anyone with eyes could tell you're a Luddite. Your watch is ancient."

"It's vintage."

"Your phone is arcane."

"It makes and receives phone calls. Anything else is superfluous to requirements. The moment I feel myself pining for a selfie stick I'll upgrade. She also did something to your computer."

Jonathon's face lit up. "As in…?"

"After rolling her eyes at the screen so often I thought she'd burst a blood vessel suddenly she was done. Twenty-four hours of videos finished in a morning."

Jonathon barked with laughter. "Told you I can pick them."

"Why are you smiling? She cheated."

"She's industrious."

"You act as if this is a trifling consideration. She is the kind of character I would usually be hired to uncover, not someone I would ever choose to work alongside."

Jonathon waited for Armand to finish his denouncement. "You done?"

"Quite."

"Did she sit back and stare at the ceiling once she was done...?" Jonathon waved a hand.

"Being industrious?" Armand helped. "She did not."

"Did she pretend to work while surreptitiously checking her phone?"

No, and neither did she appear furtive or nervous. Check over her shoulder or blink excessively. All signs of guilt. "She appeared utterly delighted with herself. Then asked to be put to work."

Jonathon held out his hands in supplication before his phone rang.

"A moment," said Jonathan, holding up a finger. He pressed a button and took a call, leaving Armand with his thoughts.

Armand brought out his phone. He did indeed have one. Though he mainly used it to ignore concerned messages from his family back in Paris who were terrified he was working on something dangerous.

He wasn't a technophobe, as Evie had declared. He'd built a ham radio while at uni. Fixed a walkie-talkie once in the middle of a mortar attack.

His brain worked better with the tactile feel of paper and pencil in hand. No doubt an echo of growing up in a family of art lovers, gallery owners, generations of Debussey auctioneers, where the senses were meant for the appreciation of beauty, form, history, not for looking into a person's eyes, peeling back layers of their soul and seeing to their darkest heart.

"Everything okay?" Jonathon asked.

Tired of having to assure people he was "fine", Armand didn't deign to answer. He stood. Said, "What now?"

"Regarding…?"

"Ms Croft."

"I meant it when I said that is entirely up to you. Whatever it takes for you to get to the bottom of whatever the hell is wrong with my shiny new app. It's the only reason I brought you here after all."

"Really? From memory you brought me here

because… Let me try to bring up the exact words. I was 'wasting away in my big, ivy-covered chateau like some tragic hero in a gothic novel'."

"Heroine. I believe I used the word heroine."

Armand moved to the door.

"Evie can help you, Armand. If you don't believe me, kick her to the kerb."

With that Jonathon pressed another button on his desk and took another call, and this time Armand walked away and kept going, all the way to his room at the end of the hall.

The door was shut, but he could hear noise from within. A throb, like a heartbeat. He pressed his thumb onto the discreet pad and the lock clicked open.

In the short time she'd been back from her break, Evie had made herself at home. She'd figured out the lamps had dimmers and had switched them all to bright. She'd plugged her phone into a tiny speaker in the shape of a pineapple, and it was pumping out music.

She'd pulled her hair into a messy knot on top of her head and it bounced from side to side as she swayed on her feet, fingers tapping over her keyboard. The light from the monitors shining on her contented face.

And the whole room smelled like cherries.

"Ms Croft. Evie."

Clearly not having heard him enter, she nearly jumped out of her boots, her short skirt flapping and swishing around the tops of her long legs. In the brighter light the instant rush of pink to her cheeks was clear.

She pressed something on her phone and the music went dead. "I saw you in Jonathon's office. Am I fired?"

"Did you do something that would make that a concern?"

She held up the Post-it note. In his handwriting it read, "Finish the training videos."

"I believe Jonathon would have been disappointed if you hadn't found a way around them."

She held a hand to her chest as she laughed, clearly relieved. "I get why HR would insist— it's the age of the lawsuit after all. But he needs to invest in better videos."

"Feel free to tell him."

"Did you have to watch them?"

Armand breathed out before saying, "Of course."

She pointed a finger his way and laughed. "Liar!"

He'd held eye contact. He'd not shifted his feet. His nostrils had not flared. Every sign of lying subjugated by years of specialised training in the Legion. And yet she'd seen through him.

He could tell himself his heart had not speeded up, his hands did not sweat. Those feelings, that level of care, had been worn down to the nub.

Which had nothing at all to do with his change of subject. "Your lunch companion seemed fond of you."

"Jamie? No. Do you think?"

"There was no need to think. He made it perfectly clear."

"How? No. Don't tell me. It wouldn't matter if he was...fond."

"And why not?"

"Work and play don't mix. Lines become blurred. Trust misconstrued. Boundaries breeched. And when things fall apart..." Evie turned her fist into a bomb which exploded with accompanying sound effects.

Her mouth quirked. Such a pretty mouth. Light, soft, prone to laughter.

"You Australians are too uptight," Armand chided. "In France such things are not a concern. Lovers are found where they are found. In a bar, at a party, at work. The location is merely scenery."

"Right," she said, her huge brown eyes no longer blinking. Instead they held on to his in such a way he found it hard to disengage. "I'll make sure to remember that."

Growling, mostly beneath his breath, he said, "Would you like to know what you are going to do with all that stuff or not?"

Instantly deflected, she placed her hands on either side of a screen as if covering a pair of sensitive ears. "This stuff, I'll have you know, is beyond your wildest imaginings. Yes, I would like to know what I am going to be doing with all this stuff!"

"You signed the confidentiality agreement?"

Her eyes narrowed, temper crackling. "Of course I did."

All that energy, Armand thought. Was there ever a time when he'd burned with such passion? About anything good?

He held out a hand, motioning to the lounge. She took one end, he took the other. A face-off.

"Jonathon has recently purchased a start-up app and wishes for us to give it a once-over before it launches."

Evie was up, moving back to the middle of the room, where she stretched her arms over her head, did a small pirouette before stopping and pinning him with those dark eyes of hers. "He's already bought it?"

Armand nodded.

"And now he wants me to have a look?"

"Yes."

"That's like buying a house and then checking for termites."

"I believe I have mentioned Jonathon can be reckless when over-excited."

"Any one of the guys downstairs could check the code, could Beta-test. Why would he need me? Armand?"

"Yes, Evie."

"Does Montrose's shiny new app have termites?"

"We believe so."

Evie slapped her hands together, then had the good grace to look chagrined. "It's not uncommon. No program is perfect. Unless... Unless he's concerned that the problem is systemic. Or deliberate. Is that why he has us holed up here? He believes his app was sabotaged?"

Armand ran a hand over the bristle on his chin, chiding himself on how staunchly he'd resisted. It was time to stop thinking of her in terms of her relative youth. Her innocence. Just because he'd lived a dozen more lifetimes than she had, it did not diminish her resourcefulness, her value.

"Jeez," she said, pacing now. "Who would do such a thing?"

"People whose proposals he has rejected. People whose companies he has bought and dismantled. Competitors. Anonymous..."

"Okay. I get it. You've had to cast the net wide."

"You have no idea."

"If I'm finding termites, what's your part in all this?"

"I figure out who put them there and why."

"How?"

"My background is in history. Finance. Law. I talk to people. Comb through online chatter, phone records, bank statements." Mostly above board. A man with his responsibilities had to do what he had to do. "They'll have given themselves away at some point. Via a pay-out, a boast in a pub, a line in a contract. Everyone does."

She glanced over his shoulder to the pile of folders on his desk, the legal books on the shelves behind. "Clever. A little scary, but impressive. And you've been doing all this on your own?"

He nodded.

She twisted her fingers together. Cracked a few

knuckles. "Well, you're not alone anymore. Point the way, partner."

Armand felt a skitter of something flicker to life behind his ribs. He wouldn't go so far as calling it zeal, or gusto, but it was something. An echo. A memory. The thrill of the hunt. "What do you need?"

Her mouth curved into a Cheshire cat grin. "Nothing that's not already there. Programmers always leave breadcrumbs. Snail trails. Their personal signature. If they've left tracks I'll find them. Wow, I sounded pretty fierce just now. I bet you're not used to that kind of talk in your field."

Before he even felt the words coming they came. "Ah, but I wasn't always the dashing paper pusher you see before you. Not all that long ago I worked in search and rescue."

Evie stopped her pacing and slowly sat on the armrest, drinking him in like a sponge. "You? How?"

"A family friend's little girl had gone missing."

"Come on, you can't leave me hanging. What happened? How on earth did you get involved?"

Realising he'd put himself in it, Armand saw only one way out: the truth.

"I'd had...experience tracking bad people down. My father's friends begged my family to ask me to help. I put together a team of colleagues from my previous employ whom I believed would have the requisite skills, the emotional stamina, the trustworthiness. For her father was prominent. French government. A good man, with divisive left-wing views. The chances of recovery, even if we tracked her, were slim."

"Then what?" Evie asked, her face grim, her voice a mite breathless. "Please tell me there's a happy ending coming."

"We—as you said—followed the breadcrumbs and recovered the little girl in less than twenty-four hours. Alive. Unhurt. Happy ending."

For all his covertness word had spread through the highest echelons of power. Problem on the down-low? He was the man to fix it. Without even meaning to, Armand had built himself a posse of men like him: skilled but untethered, having witnessed a lot of bad and now looking to do some good.

And it had been good. The perfect blend of his experience and education.

No matter how hard he tried to cap the recollection there, to the good times, his mind flowed to its logical conclusion. To Lucia. The little girl's aunt. They'd met the day he'd brought her niece home. Coolly beautiful, polished, and from a family as venerated as his own, she would, he'd believed, be his way back to the real world. He'd been wrong.

"Wow, Armand," said Evie on an outward breath, her husky voice tugging him gently back to the present. "You're a real-life hero. You and your Action Adventure All-Stars."

Armand shook his head. "No more than anyone with skills who knows how to use them."

"Come on. You're allowed to feel a little smug. You did that! You saved a girl."

She was so chuffed at the thought, Armand felt a smile tug at the edges of his eyes. It caught, ached, as if those muscles had not been used in a very long time. He didn't realise he was sitting forward, leaning in, until he breathed in and caught the scent of cherry.

He rubbed both hands over his face before pulling his heavy body to standing then walked purposefully back to his desk and sat.

All the while thinking, *Breadcrumbs. Snail trails.*

Every life followed a path. Straight, meandering, going around in circles. Paths that were broad and gentle or treacherous and overstretched. Paths that were halted by sudden mountains, the traveller stopped, stymied, stuck before finding a way over, or around. Or not.

It made sense that computer programs—programmed by humans—would be the same. It made sense that Evie, knowing the terrain, would be able to follow the map and find Jonathon's mountain. Leaving Armand to find out who'd put it there.

He'd planned to give Evie only pieces of the puzzle, to ensure the security of the project. Now he found himself saying, "Blue icon."

Like a team member he'd worked with a hundred times, she had his shorthand down. She bounded back to her desk and beamed at the screen. "Got it."

He gave her the password. She typed it in and waggled her fingers as she waited for it to load.

He saw the moment she noted the name of the program. Not so much a new start-up app as Game On—Jonathon's new flagship telecommunications software. The one the entire country was waiting for.

Evie turned to him with comically wide eyes. "Are you kidding me?"

Armand shook his head.

Then watched as a calm came over Evie. As she breathed in and out. As she pressed her feet into the ground and shook the jitters from her hands. He'd seen those moves more times than he could count. She was preparing herself for battle.

"I can do this, Armand."

"I don't doubt it," he said, and meant it.

For the next several minutes they worked in silence—Evie tapping away, fingers flying over her customised keyboard, the mouse. Face a study in concentration.

Armand tried to find his rhythm. Marking up red flags in correspondence between Jonathon's lawyers and the company from whom he'd bought the base software. But he couldn't settle. "How's it going?"

Glints of gold snapped in her big brown eyes as she turned them on him. "No termites as yet, if that's what you wanted to hear."

Armand wasn't exactly sure what he wanted, so he let it go.

But after a few seconds, Evie asked, "If I'm the Exterminator, then what do we call you?"

"Armand will do just fine."

"Come on," she said, half closing one eye. "A title gives you focus. Even Napoleon wanted to be Emperor. So who are you?"

Evie couldn't possibly know how much that question had weighed on him his whole life. Who was he? A Debussey. A scholar. An art historian. Yes, but also a foot soldier. An enforcer. A leader. A helper. A shadow. A blade. Until the day he'd realised that even the most determined, most skilled, most focussed fighter for good could be brought to their knees by bad luck.

Right now he was a friend doing a friend a favour.

And to do that well he needed a partner on the mission. For that was what she was. Her knowledge of the playing field was stronger than his.

He'd believed Jonathon had given him this young woman as a move in one of his games. But there was far more to her than exuberance and a knack for being underestimated. Armand felt a flicker of self-reproach, when he'd thought he was done with feeling much at all.

He cleared his throat. "You can call me the Undertaker."

Evie laughed, the sound husky and sure. Then she shot him a sideways glance.

Another very different sliver of sensation shimmered to life in parts of him he'd thought were nothing but dust motes, pain and remorse.

She said, "I'll kill the problem and you'll bury it?"

"Something like that."

"Okay, then." She cocked her head and got back to work.

Her quiet focus became magnetic, as if she'd drawn all that cracking energy back inside of her. Headphones back on her head, she rocked from side to side.

Armand craned his head to listen. But it was a song he didn't know. A song young people liked. Young Australian people with no cares in the world.

When Armand realised he was staring he took his subconscious by the throat and gave it a good shake. Now was not the time for distraction. He'd been skirting around the edges of the playing field until today. Now it was game on.

He grabbed his paperwork and began to read.

Evie jiggled her key in the door of Zoe's apartment, bumped the door open with her shoulder and threw her backpack, beanie and scarf onto the futon before collapsing into a heap with a sigh.

"Work was that good, huh?" asked Zoe.

Evie lifted her eyes to find her flatmate standing in the door of her bedroom, one leg hooked up on the other knee, eating tuna from the tin.

Voice muffled by a cushion, Evie said, "It was amazing."

The code she'd been hired to investigate was brilliant. Elegant and clean. So neat it shone. Meaning any kind of error ought to stand out like a lump of coal. But the best part of her day? When she'd been gifted a glimpse behind Armand's hard outer shell to the private man beneath.

Zoe said, "Tell me all about it."

"The job itself... I can't talk about."

Zoe rolled her eyes. "Used to that."

"For all the laid-back, geek-boy first impression, the infrastructure is slick. Sharp. Fast. And the technology we are working with... I think I'm in love. No, I'm definitely in love."

"And the people?"

With the word *love* ringing in her ears, and Armand's deep voice rumbling in his ear as he told her about the time he'd saved that little girl... She cleared her throat. "Men. Pretty much all men."

"Lucky you."

"You think?"

Zoe loped back into the kitchenette. "Yeah, I get it. For me, in fashion, it's pretty much the opposite. Anytime we get a man at work, gay or straight, the poor guy's mobbed. Any particular men we need to talk about?"

Evie tried to pull up Jamie's face, but all she got was light hair, teeth, a general air of flirtation. Then the vague image instantly morphed into dark angles and stormy blue eyes. Elegant slouch and constant scowl. A ridiculously sexy accent saying, "*Lovers are found where they are found...*"

"Nope," Evie said. "Not a one."

Zoe slapped herself on the head. "I'd nearly forgotten. What about Mr Lonely Heart?"

Which was when Evie realised she'd forgotten to tell Zoe that whole tale. And there was no way she could see around it. Squeezing one eye shut, she said, "Turns out he works for Game Plan too."

Zoe's eyes near popped out of her head. "Noooo. Wow. That's...fate."

"Yes... No." She told Zoe about the book, the folders. "A simple case of subliminal messaging."

"But what about the lonely heart...?"

"Not him." She was almost one hundred percent sure.

"Bummer."

"It's a good thing. Means we can have a normal working relationship—cool, distant, professional." Evie rolled off the futon and landed on her hands and knees before crawling into the bathroom, where she started up a hot bath.

Then, a moment later, Zoe's voice came through the keyhole. "If it wasn't him, then who? Any man who writes poetry should be given a chance."

Evie reached into the bath and turned the taps to full blast, the noise of the spray giving her the excuse not to answer.

# CHAPTER FIVE

THE NEXT MORNING Zoe and Evie sat in their usual seats on the train.

It was a gorgeous Melbourne winter's day—crisp blue skies and a brisk chill in the air. Yet Evie felt warm. Scratchy. She took off her bright red bomber jacket, then put it back on again. She fiddled with her beanie—black today, with double pom-poms that looked like teddy-bear ears. And she tried to stop staring at the electronic sign telling them how many stops to Armand's South Yarra stop.

Thankfully, Zoe was too busy sexting Lance, who'd landed back in Australia after his final overseas army posting. A few days, then, till Evie had to find somewhere else to live.

She rocked forward as the train came to a halt. Her eyes zoomed to the doors. And a familiar form filled the space like liquid darkness.

Cool, distant, professional, she told herself. But, as Armand's eyes swept over the carriage before landing on hers, her nerves zapped and zinged, the hairs on her arms standing on end.

Zoe's hand flapped in the corner of Evie's vision as she waved for Armand to join them.

"Zoe," Evie hissed. "Leave him be."

"You're kidding, right?"

Eyes still locked onto Armand, Evie saw the squaring of his shoulders before he excused himself as he made his way up the busy aisle.

"Good morning, Evie."

"Hey, Armand. Um, this is my friend Zoe. Zoe, Armand."

Zoe held out a hand and shook Armand's with relish. "Sit."

The schoolboys must have had a day off, as there was a spare seat across from them. While Armand settled in Evie rearranged herself so as not to spend the trip playing footsie with the guy.

Zoe said, "I hear you two are working together."

Evie caught Armand's gaze, inscrutable as ever. "I only mentioned we were working together, not what we're working on."

Zoe scoffed. "I wouldn't understand it anyway."

"She really wouldn't. Then again, neither would Armand."

Armand's intense gaze darkened, just a fraction. It was quite the thing.

After three solid seconds of eye contact, his gaze swept to Zoe. "She thinks I'm a Luddite."

"I thought you were French. Didn't you say he's French?"

"I did. He is." Evie's mouth kicked into a grin and Armand's eyes seemed to spark in shared amusement. A secret shared. Evie's heart took a little tumble.

She swallowed quickly and turned to Zoe—much safer—to explain the history of the Luddites and their aversion to new technology.

The conversation then moved on to the design program Zoe was being forced to learn for work, to when it might be cold enough for proper coats, to the underfloor heating in Armand's penthouse apartment in South Yarra.

"Posh," Zoe said. "Does it have an extra bedroom?"

It took Evie a moment to break free from the Zen of listening to Armand talk and realise where Zoe was going. She gave her friend an elbow in the ribs.

"Ouch. It's a perfectly reasonable question." Zoe sat forward. "Beneath the cool exterior, our girl here is brimming with panic as she is under the mistaken impression she has to move out of my place this week."

"She mentioned she was moving," Armand said.

"My boyfriend is moving in, so she thinks she has to leave."

"It's a one-bedroom place. I sleep on a futon in the lounge. When Lance moves in it will be a little…"

"Cramped," Evie said right as Armand joined in with,

"Intimate."

"That too," Evie said, her voice a little rough. Their eyes locked. Evie swallowed. So much for "cool, distant, professional".

Taking Armand's loaded silence for disapproval, Zoe added, "Don't worry. It won't distract her from work."

He shook his head, his mussed hair unsettling and resettling in an even more appealing alignment. "I've seen her work. It would take an airstrike siren to distract her."

Zoe laughed. "And you've only known her a day. I wish my boss saw me like that. I've been working there a year and a half and she still thinks my name is Zelda." Zoe nodded towards the door. "Your stop, guys."

Armand stood.

This time Evie knew better than to try to keep up, so she made a play out of slowly collecting her things.

"Don't be late," he instructed. Then with a nod he was gone.

Evie saluted his back, then scrambled to get her backpack from under the seat.

"I like him," said Zoe as Evie stepped over her legs.

"Then you can have him."

Not wanting to look as if she was following Armand, Evie had dawdled to work. In the end she ran late, puffing by the time she reached the Bullpen.

Naturally the first person she banged into was her boss.

"Mr Montrose!"

"Evie. How goes it? Settling in all right? Making friends? Getting the lie of the land?"

"Great!" she enthused. "All is great!"

"I see. Armand has scared you witless, has he?"

Evie laughed. "He's rather intense." *Arrogant,*

*short-tempered, closed-off. Mysterious, hunky, fascinating.*

"Can be. Comes from being a genius among mere mortals."

"Then how come you're so nice?"

Jonathon blinked, then looked at her. Really looked at her for the first time since they had met. *Notice me. See me. And please don't fire me.*

Thankfully he laughed. "You'll keep."

He looked ready to move on when he turned back to her. "Keep me in the loop, Evie."

"Of course."

"Not merely apropos the investigation. With regards to Armand."

Evie swallowed, not quite sure how to answer. "I'm not sure I understand."

"The usual. If he's playing nice, if he's giving you enough space to do your job, how goes his state of mind."

"State of mind?"

Jonathon glanced over her shoulder, the very image of nonchalant. "Has he spoken much about his life before he came here?"

Apart from the story about the little girl, he'd barely spoken at all. "We've mostly talked about the work."

"Is he settling in? Making friends?"

*Help.*

The only time she'd seen him interact with anyone was when he'd glared down at Jamie at lunch. "I can't really say."

A flash of a smile. "You're loyal to him already. Good to see."

Was it loyalty? Or the fact she didn't know him at all?

Suddenly Evie's stomach tightened and her ears began to burn as she remembered a similar conversation with her last boss, asking her how things were going with Eric. On that occasion she'd completely misunderstood—blustering over the fact that they'd broken up, kind of, that they were in the process of moving on, not realising her boss was asking if she'd noticed anything untoward.

Not that Armand seemed *anything* like Eric. Polar opposite, in fact.

Eric had been affable, like a St Bernard puppy. He'd appeared harmless and wasn't.

While Armand... He was far more at the Doberman pinscher end of the scale. A stunning specimen, but instinct said it was best not to stray too close. And yet he read actual books. Stood on the train so old ladies could sit. Had seemed gen-

uinely concerned—in his own intangible way—
that she might soon be out on her ear.

Before she could come to any logical conclu-
sions, Jonathon gave her a nod and left her to
hurry to her office.

She went to press her thumbprint against the
security pad, only to find it was missing, the door
unlocked and Armand working on the security
pad, coloured cords poking out every which way.

She edged in behind him, intrigued. Electrical
circuits were one of the first things her granddad
had taught her about when he'd realised it was
easier to answer her zillion questions than hope
they'd go away on their own.

Making to "play nice", she went to point out
he had the wrong micro-screwdriver, when he
reached into a small toolbox and pulled out the
right one.

The man might not know a gigabyte from a bug
bite, but he clearly was capable in countless other
ways. Of course, it only served to make him even
more intriguing when she really needed him to
become less.

He grunted. Then said something in… Swed-
ish? She realised he was also on the phone. A
regular old landline tucked between ear and
shoulder.

But it was the tone of his voice that was the biggest surprise. It could almost be mistaken for chipper.

She glanced towards Jonathon's office, wondering if she ought to tell him. But it didn't feel right. If Jonathon wanted them to get along, then she'd make it her focus to get along.

She caught Armand's eye as she moved to her desk to let him know she'd arrived. He gave her a small nod as she passed—practically a hug in Armand world.

Then stopped when she found a new addition to her little corner—a small cabinet, elegant, wooden, most likely antique, with enough room for her backpack and a shelf for personal touches she'd brought from home. And, above, a pair of fat knobs nailed to the wall, the perfect size for her scarf. And her beanie.

She turned to ask Armand if he knew who to thank but stopped short when she saw him leaning back in his chair, ankle hooked over the opposite knee, a hand waving through the air as he illustrated some point the person on the other end of the line could not see.

It was the smile that got her. Wide, crooked, creasing the edges of his eyes until they were no longer stormy. Her blood rushed so hard and fast she could hear it in her ears.

Gaze sweeping unseeingly over the room, those eyes caught on hers. A mercurial, sparkling blue-grey, like sunlight on water.

The swinging stopped. His hand dropped. The smile slowly melted away.

But the light in his eyes remained. Just for a moment. A breath really. But enough for something to rage to life deep in Evie's belly.

Then he blinked, his gaze sliding away from her as if it had never caught, his chair turned to face the other wall as he continued his discourse, the foreign words quieting, easing down the phone lines.

Evie sat. Switched on her computer. Got to work. But it was a while before her heart slowed. Before she could even see the screen.

A half-hour later she jumped when Armand said, in English this time, "Team meeting."

She turned to find him at the lounge. The halfway mark of the office. No-man's-land.

Evie played with the zip on her bomber jacket as she moved out to join him. Then sat primly on the edge of the couch. Her hands clasped together.

Armand said, "You go first."

"Who was on the phone?"

He baulked. "A colleague."

"A colleague…?"

"Performing background checks."

She waited for more, to get some insight into who in his life could make him smile that way. But nope. She got nothing. "Have they found anything to report?"

His eyebrow jumped.

Evie brought her hand to her chest. "Or am I not allowed to ask?"

Armand's inscrutable gaze flickered and she half expected him to say, no, she was not allowed to ask.

In the end he waved a conciliatory hand and went on to outline the work he'd done so far. The accounting errors that seemed just that. The dead ends he'd reached. The players he was targeting as suspicious. It was an impressive amount of work. She wondered that he'd had time to sleep, much less settle in, make friends.

"I bumped into Jonathon this morning," she said when he was done.

"And?"

"He asked me to keep him in the loop."

Armand stilled. No, he stiffened, his entire body going rigid. But his voice was smooth, giving nothing away as he said, "It is his business."

"It wasn't about the *business*. He asked me to keep an eye on you."

Armand shot to his feet, pacing back and forth over the same small patch of floor, muttering in French and a little English about "trust" and "allegiance", with a few choice swear words thrown in for flavour. It was more emotion than she had ever seen him display—anger, disappointment, regret. The mix volatile, unexpected; she couldn't hope to pin each down.

Evie stood, running suddenly sweating palms down the front of her jacket. "Armand, I told you because I have no intention of following through."

Armand stopped mid-stride. "What do you mean?"

"The way I see it, we are a team. If one of us is playing the other it won't work. Been there, done that, don't ever want to go through it again. But if I'm wrong, if this is more than Jonathon stirring, if there's something about you I should know..."

Armand pinned her with a dark glare. "You said it yourself—we are a team. We are not friends. There is nothing you need to know bar the report I just gave."

The burn travelled fast, singeing her cheeks till they flared. She held up both hands in surrender. "Forget I said anything."

He gave her one last, long look before he walked slowly to his chair, where he sat and watched her from his place in the semi-darkness.

Evie crossed her arms. "I take it the team meeting is over?"

Armand waved a hand in agreement before he scraped his fingernails through his stubble.

Evie scooted back to her own desk, where she sat, stiff-backed, staring unseeingly at her monitors.

A few moments later, Armand's voice came to her. "If this job is so important to you, why not do as Jonathon asked? Why tell me at all?"

She turned, keeping her fingers poised on the keyboard. "I didn't think it was fair." One thing she had taken out of the implosion of her last job and her part in it was that whatever happened she had to be able to live with herself.

Armand sank his face into his hands a moment before giving it a good scrub and looking at her with haunted eyes. "Bad things happen to good people in this world. I've seen it time and time again. If you don't toughen up, grow a thicker skin, I fear for you, Evie. I really do."

"If you'd prefer to sit over there in the darkness, glowering at nothing, keeping whatever has Jonathon so concerned all bottled up inside, you're going to have a stroke. I fear for you, Armand. I really do."

She glared at him and he glared back. When her eyes began to water at the stalemate she blinked, rolled her eyes and got back to work.

Her fingers slammed down on the keyboard, till she remembered it was her beloved prototype and took more care. Mind spinning in a dozen different directions, she forced herself to concentrate. To curb her anger. To do her job.

But, as the code finally drew her in, one niggling little thought kept flashing at the corner of her mind.

Evie might not know much about why people acted the way they did, but she did know family. She knew community. She knew fellowship.

She hadn't felt much of that in her last job. They had valued her but only for the skills she offered. They'd rated her so highly they'd stuck her in a secure office where no one bar top management—and Eric—could visit. Rather than feel appreciated, she'd felt isolated. Like a tool rather than a human being.

Armand said he feared for her, which meant she wasn't merely a cog in the corporate machine to him. To him, at least, she mattered.

She settled in with a small smile on her face,

feeling as if they might not turn out to be the worst partnership ever assembled after all.

Evie's stomach rumbled.

After their earlier standoff, the office was deathly quiet. Armand must have heard. But when she looked up it was to find him in his regularly programmed position—frowning over his reports, the pool of golden light cast by the banker's lamp throwing craggy shadows over his deep, soulful eyes.

*This man worries about me. He'd care if something terrible happened to me.*

Armand looked up and Evie started at having been caught staring.

"Did you bring lunch?" she blurted.

"Lunch?" he asked, as if he'd never heard of such a concept that might take time away from glaring at paperwork. "*Non.*"

Even while she wasn't playing his game, Jonathon had hit on something when asking if Armand had made friends. She knew how it felt being the odd one out at work. Just because she'd decided not to report back, it didn't mean she couldn't help.

"I'm heading down to the Yum Lounge to

find something decadent and delicious to eat."
A pause, a deep breath, then, "Care to join me?"

Armand looked up, those dark eyes bringing
on tingles and skitters and rising heat. Then he
surprised the heck out of her by shutting his notebook and saying, "*Oui*, I will. *Merci*."

"Really? Great. Okay. Let's go."

Evie held out a hand, motioning to the door. But
Armand refused to go before her, waiting with
barely reined patience for her to trot through.

Once out of the office, Armand locked the door,
even though the security key pad meant that only
select people had access anyway. No trust, that
man. Since reading people wasn't her forte, she
gave everyone the benefit of the doubt. Probably
best he was in charge.

As they reached the Bullpen the energy, the
laughter, the sense of chaos couldn't have been
more different from the intense quiet of upstairs.
She glanced towards Armand to find him tense,
bristling, on high alert. For a moment it was easy
to picture him as he might have once been, not
hunting a problem, but the kind of man who'd
take care of a scared little girl.

She shot him a smile. Turned it into a grin.
Gave him a nudge with her elbow.

While his face said he was still considering her

sanity, his shoulders relaxed and the tendons in his neck no longer looked like they might burst from his skin.

When he took a turn towards the Yum Lounge, Evie grabbed his wrist. He froze, as if shocked by human touch. Making a split-second decision, she slid her fingers into his and dragged him towards the Game Rooms, stopping when she found Jamie and a couple of colleagues battling it out to get past what looked like the penultimate level of *Insurgent: Jungle Fever III.*

She called out, "Hey, guys."

Several heads turned. Some waved, others raised cans of energy drink. When some looked warily over her shoulder she glanced back at Armand, realising she was still holding his hand.

She let go. His hand immediately sank into the pocket of his suit pants. Then she tipped her head in the direction of the room, prompting him to acknowledge the crowd.

"These guys are on our team too," she murmured.

He muttered something in French. She did not believe it was complimentary.

"You guys game?" someone called.

"Totally," Armand responded.

Laughter bursting from her mouth, she turned

to find Armand had moved in closer. She rolled her shoulders, subtly, in an attempt to stave off the warmth washing over her at his nearness.

Jamie, who was sitting in a straight-backed chair, fingers flying over a controller, sweat beading on his forehead, didn't move as he said, "Miss Evie, nice to see you down here." Then, "Armand. Welcome to hell."

"Looks fairly close," Armand said, his hard gaze now locked on the huge screen where soldiers in camouflage gear, loaded up to the eyeballs in weapons, tried to shoot their way out of an ambush.

"How long have you been stuck there?" Evie asked.

"This session? Two hours and sixteen minutes."

Another guy added, "That's not including the several days before that."

"Jonathon pays you to do this?" Armand asked.

"We're about to launch *Jungle Fever IV* and need to make sure we haven't doubled up on any scenes."

"Do you use military consultants?"

One guy looked up. "My uncle was a lieutenant in Vietnam. We brought in a few of his mates to fill in the blanks."

Armand shot him a look. Gave him a single nod, appeased, before standing up straight.

Evie took a couple of steps into the room. Eyeballed the screen, catalogued the tools lists of each player. "You want help?"

Yet another guy hunched over a controller muttered, "We are beyond help. And I'm out."

He put down the controller and slumped over in the chair.

Evie held out a hand and someone passed the controller to her.

After a beat she offered it to Armand. "Care to show them how it's done?"

A flash passed over his eyes, a moment of connection, like lightning within a storm. A thrill shot down her spine, making her toes curl.

Then he slowly shook his head. "All yours."

"All righty, then," she said, taking a moment to shake off the pins and needles. She ran her fingers over the buttons, familiarising herself with the remote. Cricked her neck one way, then the other.

"Follow me," she commanded Jamie, then set to unlocking the level in a minute and a half.

The room erupted in a cheer befitting a gold medal performance.

Grinning, Evie bowed to the room, bowed to

Jamie, then turned to bow to Armand. He leaned in the doorway, arms crossed, ankles too. Cool as you please.

He shook his head once, his eyes glinting. And then his face lit up with a smile. Teeth and all. A zing shot through her, head to toe, as if she'd been struck by lightning.

Grouchy, he was magnetic.

Smiling, the man was devastating.

Out of the corner of her eye she saw Jamie throw down his controller and pull off his baseball cap to run a hand over his damp hair. "How?" he asked.

Evie broke eye contact to give Jamie a shrug. "I'm just that good."

"Everyone," Jamie said as he pulled himself to standing, "this is Evie Croft. And she is just that good."

Each of the guys stood to introduce themselves, a flurry of names she'd struggle to remember. Evie laughed, feeling light, happy. Included. It was the best she'd felt since the Day of the Fortune Cookie.

Then her gaze slid back to the doorway to find Armand's smile now gone. He glanced behind him, as if looking for a way to escape.

With an, "Excuse me," Evie ducked through the

crowd. She muttered, "Uh-uh, don't even think about it." Then, tucking her hand into his elbow, she dragged Armand bodily into the room.

Evie shook any hand that came her way and said, "And this is Armand Debussey."

Armand did surprisingly well in the end—he smiled politely, was charming despite his best efforts and was an adept conversationalist. After a few minutes, it felt as if they were all firm friends.

Fun now over, the crowd dissipated, small groups heading off in different directions, already talking about optic cables and firewalls.

"Well, that wasn't so hard, now, was it?" Evie asked, turning to Armand. "Even I started to believe you were an actual human person."

Armand smiled, just a little, and Evie found herself lost in a whirl of stormy blue. She'd never stood so close to him before, apart from elbowing him on the train. Toe to toe. Close enough to count his tangled lashes. The lines on his face that spoke of hardship, worry. Of care.

Her next breath in felt sharp and keen and far too shallow.

Her tongue slipped over her dry bottom lip and Armand's gaze dropped to her mouth. And stayed. The banked heat in his eyes had her knees giving way.

Then from one moment to the next the shutters closed over his eyes with a snap and he took an instant step back.

"Lunch?" she said, glad to remember what it was called.

He looked at her for a beat. Inscrutable once more. "No lunch. I have something urgent that needs attending to."

"Oh," she said, hearing the tinge of disappointment clear as day. "Okay. See you in the office afterwards, then."

With a nod, and a slight bow, he left the room.

Jamie sidled up to her to give her a bump with his shoulder. "Seems you're after a lunch companion."

She had to drag her eyes away from the doorway to give Jamie a chummy smile. The smile she got back was more than chummy.

While Armand was a study in elusiveness and restraint, Jamie was not. There was a strong chance she was reading the signs wrong, but she didn't think so. The smoulder he was sending her was as subtle as a billboard.

She was hit with a revelation.

What if *Jamie* was the fortune cookie mistake?

Was he the romantic entanglement she had to nip in the bud?

She felt a sudden lightness come over her. If it was true, it would be the easiest fix in the world!

He was nice-looking, smart and clearly keen, but she felt nothing for him beyond friendship. Nothing close to the way she felt when Armand even looked her way.

Suddenly her revelation didn't feel helpful after all.

"Thanks," she said to Jamie. "But I don't think that's a good idea."

His face dropped till he looked like a sad little boy and she knew she'd made the right decision.

"Look, I know I'm a novelty around here but, like you, I'm here to do my job. Just think of me as one of the guys."

Jamie perked up. "You sure played like one."

Evie bit the inside of her lip to stop herself from calling him out as a sexist pig. Hopefully she'd have the chance to show them all how wrong they were.

Jamie ran a hand up the back of his neck. "You and Mr Mysterious—you're not…?"

"God, no! No way! Nuh-uh." *Stop protesting. One "no" is plenty. Okay, one more for good measure.* "Nope. We are a project team. And that is all."

Jamie watched her a moment, then nodded. Backing away, he said, "Rematch?"

"Deal."

He shot her a salute and headed off.

Left alone in the Bullpen, Evie lifted her gaze up the stairs.

That was what she wanted, right? To quietly go about her job without making waves? Making a splash had been her mum's deal. Being lauded, applauded, recognised for her artistic talents. Her dreams had been so big that when she'd crashed she'd crashed hard.

Evie had never wanted standing ovations, she just wanted a seat at the table. And now she finally had one.

But, while half an hour before she'd been starving hungry, right then she felt strangely hollow.

# CHAPTER SIX

ARMAND SAT AT his desk, the lamp light as low as it would go.

Discomfort sat on his shoulder like a cloak—his nerves twitching with over-stimulation, making him realise how long he'd cut himself off, kept himself numb by thinking over his past, his choices, to remind himself why apathy was imperative.

Life had started well for Armand—a golden childhood spent in Saint-Germain-des-Prés, summering on the waters of the Côte d'Azur. He'd been an active child—rugby at school, excelling in track and field at university. Backpacking through Turkey with friends—including a young Jonathon Montrose—after graduation had been an easy choice. And one that had changed the course of his life.

He still remembered that day his life had flipped on a hinge with wretched clarity: late spring, bright, sunny sky. A bunch of rich kids hopping loudly off the dilapidated bus, dragging their matching luggage. To the band of rebels waiting in the rocky outcrops—their clothes tattered, their bellies empty—Armand and his friends must have looked ripe for the picking.

Armand remembered sitting on a bag, watching Jonathon chat with the bus driver, when Katrina, an American girl in their group, was suddenly grabbed from behind. Basking in the sunshine, in his lazy contentment, he'd only noted she was missing when he heard her scream.

By the time he turned, she had blood running down her face from where she'd been hit with the butt of a gun. Her eyes were rolling back in her head, her legs limp as she was dragged away.

Arms raised in the international sign of surrender, Armand went after them, shouting, begging them to let her go. He threw down his wallet, his passport, a pack of gum from his pocket.

As they yelled back in a language he did not then understand, waving their guns at him, sweat prickled on his back, his neck, his scalp. He remembered the hollow feeling in his stomach. The fact he could no longer feel his feet.

But mostly he remembered the sense of utter helplessness. He'd have followed her to the ends of the earth, offered himself in her place if it had helped. But he'd had no clue if that was the right thing to do. If it would ensure her safety or get his friend killed.

Heir to the Debussey gallery and auction-house fortune, he'd known a life of obscene wealth. He knew nothing of hardship and starvation, of soul-deep pain and fear. How dared he think he could negotiate with these people? He didn't even have the wherewithal to protect what was his.

Then Katrina was gone—tossed into the back of a truck, the vehicle bouncing over the dirt hills, heading who knew where, and Armand was left with his expensive luggage and no clue as to how to get her back.

Three days later—after a police hunt, intervention by the American Embassy and what he inferred was a monetary payment by her family—Katrina was returned; beaten, bruised, with several ribs broken and permanent hearing loss in her left ear.

She was an immigration lawyer now, in Washington. Fighting to provide food, shelter and hope to those who needed it most.

Jonathon had left Europe soon after, heading off into the wild blue yonder for a number of years, before coming home to Australia with a pile of money he'd earned doing goodness knew what, invested in start-ups and made a name for himself as a leading tech entrepreneur.

Armand had gone another way.

His family had not understood his decision to join the French Foreign Legion. They'd railed against it with all that they had. Threatening legal action, disinheritance, calling on every favour they had to bring him home.

But the Legion did not bend.

He'd joined up looking for answers. And absolution. To have the wild fury that had sent him there honed by pushing his body, his mind, to their absolute limits and beyond. Stripped bare, right down to his skin, to his basic humanity, he'd rebuilt himself. It was the only way he could have overcome the events in Turkey. What he'd faced in his own mind. He might even have stayed beyond the requisite five-year term if not for the timing of the kidnapping of a little girl.

That had been years ago now. So much had happened since.

Armand tried to remember how that felt. To be so sure about his sense of duty to his friends, his corps, his family. To be so certain that he could put measures in place to make sure those he cared for could never be hurt again.

As the swamp of memory and regret threatened to suffocate, Armand dragged himself back to the here and now.

He picked up a random piece of paper from his

desk, only to find the letters swimming before his eyes. He looked up at the shelves with the bobble-headed figurines lined up below the knitted hat hanging from a hook on the wall.

Evie's trinkets. Evie's hat.

After all he'd seen and done in his life, he found the woman's lack of self-awareness exasperating. Her complete ingenuousness, her need to introduce herself to everyone she met, even the way she moved—floating across the floor as if in a permanent daydream…she may as well be walking through life with a target on her back.

Why it bothered him so much, he could not explain. For she was not his cross to bear. He barely knew her.

She was simply too young, too green, too obstreperous. She didn't listen when she ought; her opinions were far too decided. How she'd managed to come out clean from under the rubble of her previous employment he had no idea.

The woman needed a full-time minder. Not him, though. Not his speciality.

He was a finder, not a keeper.

She required a bodyguard. Or a babysitter. Even a boyfriend would do. Again, not him. Though the thought of her with one of those fledglings downstairs made his kidneys ache.

No, a man who'd seen what he'd seen and done what he'd done was not for the likes of light, bright Evie Croft.

As if he'd conjured her out of thin air, Evie hustled through the door in a whirlwind of noise and light and energy.

"Oh, hi," she said, her wide, dark eyes taking him in.

Her legs were long in tight, torn denim and studded black boots. Dark hair streamed over the shoulders of her shiny red jacket and she looked luscious and warm, loose-limbed and effortlessly sexy.

Then she took another step and tripped over nothing. Like a fawn bumbling through a forest, snapping twigs and alerting every hunter within hearing distance she was coming their way.

Armand clenched his jaw so tight he swore he heard a tooth crack. "You all right?"

"Super," she said, fixing her hair. "Nice trip? Sure was. I'm here all week. Try the veal."

Despite himself, his mouth twitched. He wiped the evidence away with a hard swipe of his hand.

Before he'd even met her he'd believed her a sitting duck. He still did.

What he hadn't known about then was her knack for self-deprecation. The serious gumption ticking away behind her ribs. The startling scope of that brain behind those big Bambi eyes. Or how fast that particular collection of attributes would reel him in.

"Did you take care of that urgent thing you suddenly remembered you had to do?" she asked.

"Not quite." *Not even close.* "What about you? Thought you'd be at the restaurant with your friends."

"The Yum Lounge, you mean?"

"I refuse to say those words in that order."

"Spoilsport." Her eyes narrowed. "They could be your friends too if you put in the tiniest effort. But alas, you are who you are."

The fact she realised it, and accepted it, when those who were meant to be his biggest supports had struggled to do the same, only made her more damn endearing.

"Anyway, I know you haven't eaten all day, so I brought the feast to you."

And now she'd brought him food.

Evie filled the silence. "No need to thank me. It was completely self-serving. The longer you go without eating, the grumpier you get, and this is a really small room. Sit. Eat. You can go back to brooding afterwards."

Without further ado, she placed a couple of

linen napkins she'd clearly stolen from the dining room and laid them out as a tablecloth, then tipped a bunch of pastries—sweet and savoury—and whole fruits into the middle.

She then nabbed a couple of cushions from the couch and tossed them on the floor. She kneeled down on one, the low lamp light catching the side of her face. Those deep, dark eyes. Full lips gently pursed as she hummed under her breath. Not a single worry line marring her pale skin.

Like a moth to a flame he pressed away from the desk, pulled up a cushion and sat. Cross-legged. As if he was in preschool. Before he could demur, the scents curled beneath his nose and his hunger got the better of him.

He picked up a mini-quiche, paused with it near his mouth as he said, "Thank you."

She passed him a serviette then smiled at him with her eyes, her mouth full of chocolate croissant.

"I don't brood. Just by the by."

She chewed. Swallowed. "You're kidding, right?"

He waited.

"You sit at your desk and frown at those papers all day long. I bet the farm you were doing exactly the same for the few weeks before I got here."

She lifted onto her knees and bent over the table to get another chocolate croissant the same time as he reached for one. When he pulled his hand away she grabbed it, turned it over, plonked the croissant within it. Then went back to grab another for herself.

The feel of her hand wrapped around his, even for the briefest moment in time, burned like a brand.

Armand had been brought up in a family who showed affection through patent family pride. They were not huggers. His work in the military and later private security had hardly changed that.

But Evie was a hugger. A toucher. And it wasn't flirtatious. Not always. Not with everyone. Though, despite knowing how very different they were, there was something there—interest, intrigue, whatever one might call that glowing filament of fascination that burned between them.

He acknowledged it, but he would not act on it. Too many people he'd let past the outer shell had paid the price.

"Eat," Evie insisted. "Before I start turning into one of my granddad's lady friends, clucking about him not looking after himself."

"I'm eating," Armand growled.

"Good. Because whatever you were thinking about just now, you've unlocked another level of brooding," she said around a mouth full of pastry.

Armand leaned over the table to get a mini-pie. And looked up to find Evie's face close to his. Closer than it had ever been.

He'd never before noticed the spot of pure gold in her left eye. Or the freckle beneath her right. He was close enough to spot the pastry crumb stuck to her bottom lip. Before he even felt himself move Armand reached out, held her chin in his hand and used the edge of his thumb to wipe it away.

The flake fluttered to the table but his hand remained, cupping her chin.

Her skin was velvet-soft, and so very warm. Exactly as he'd imagined it would be.

Because, dammit, he had imagined. The feel of her, the taste of those sweet lips. How it might feel to wake up to that smile.

Her top teeth bit down on the spot where the crumb had been, looking for more crumbs. Or to ease the sensation where contact had been made. Either way she left a liquid sheen in its wake.

Eyes glued to her mouth, Armand once more grazed his thumb over the spot. Her smooth lip tugged against his calloused thumb. Heat swarmed through him in a sudden rush.

His eyes lifted to hers to find them huge and gleaming. A pulse beat by her temple.

This was no filament of attraction; it was a wildfire.

Armand dropped his hand away.

Evie's instant intake of breath was loud in the loaded silence. She opened her mouth to say something, but Armand held up a hand.

"Eat," he said.

She frowned. Paused. Then nodded.

And so they ate.

When she went for a third chocolate croissant Armand shoved a bowl of strawberries her way.

She shot him a look. A smile. A glimmer of challenge. Before she chose a strawberry and ate it whole. He'd never seen a person smile so widely with a mouthful of food.

Looking at her, you'd never know she'd lost her job and been under investigation for embezzlement a week earlier. She'd have no place to live a week from now. Her problems, as he knew them, weren't small. And yet it didn't show.

She left them outside the office door and got on with getting on.

While he—older, wiser, having been through

so much and come out the other side relatively intact—brooded. Not unlike an infamous French beast, best known for shutting himself away in his impenetrable castle, believing himself cursed.

Enough was enough. He could do better. Be better.

Armand stood, brushed himself off.

"So soon?" she asked.

"We are no closer to an answer now than I was the day I arrived. So we work."

"Armand," Evie said, from her spot on the floor. "Despite the occasional sidestep into whimsy, I am serious about this job. Whatever problem there is, I will find it. You will believe in me enough to recommend to Jonathon that I stay on."

She looked pure in the half-light, innocent and unspoilt, but the things she was saying between the lines were not. She was setting boundaries. Telling him she felt it too—this gravity drawing them together. But her job was her number-one focus.

It should have been a relief.

When Evie slowly reached out and grabbed another croissant, Armand unexpectedly felt laughter bubble into his throat. "How can you fit any more in?"

"It's sustenance," she said. "Now, stop watching me eat and go put your brooding to good use. We have work to do."

Armand nodded once more and went back to his desk.

And even while his awareness of the woman on the other side of the small room had deepened into a constant warm glow, the letters on the pages, the numbers in the columns, the tangled concepts were suddenly sharper, clearer.

Whatever was wrong with Jonathon's deal, Armand would unearth it. For that was what he did. That was who he was.

Whether on a battlefield or in a boardroom, Armand was a man who protected his own.

Several hours later Armand sat forward, fisting his knuckles into his eye sockets.

Even with the new clarity of purpose, he felt no closer to finding the reason for Jonathon's concern bar a few items the tax office might wish to look at, but he wasn't working for them.

He looked up to find Evie pacing along the back wall, stretching out her shoulders and bouncing on the balls of her feet like a prize fighter warming up. Her hair had been piled up into a messy bun, her huge headphones were tucked over her ears and she mouthed the words to whatever song was playing.

As if she felt him watching her, she glanced over.

She stopped, hunched as she tipped the headphones backwards till they hung around her neck. And even in the semi-darkness of their cave he knew her cheeks had pinked.

"Sorry, did you say something?"

Armand shook his head.

"Anything I can do?"

"How much do you know about finance law?"

"Not a lot. But I'm a quick learner. How much do you know? Between rescuing little girls, brooding and learning multiple languages, I can't see how you manage to do anything else."

"I managed. Law and Economics at university with a side-note in Art History."

"Well, that's kind of random."

"Not when your family run a series of art auction houses."

"You're one of *those* Debusseys? I know as much about fine art as you know about debugging, but even I've heard of them. Of you."

Armand bowed with a flourish.

"Why aren't you over in Paris doing this kind of thing for them?"

He'd spent the past year doing just that and it had sucked the life out of him. Or so he'd thought.

"Long story."

"I'll bet." With a smile she grabbed her laptop and sat cross-legged on the couch.

Armand stood; the crick in his shoulder and the ache in his legs felt good. Great even. As if his whole body was grateful for the chance to be of use.

He gave his desk a quick tidy and picked up his briefcase. "Evie."

"Hmm?" Evie balanced the laptop on her knees, finger scrolling quickly over her mouse, gaze like a laser on the screen.

"It's well after six. Time to go home."

"Can't."

Something in her voice flipped a switch in Armand's gut. "What have you found?"

She shrugged one shoulder. "Nothing. Maybe something. I didn't want to say until I was sure. A thorn. Or a knot. I can't tell which. Either way I'm snagged, and I'd like to keep going while I'm on a roll. Is that allowed?"

"It's encouraged. But you haven't had a break in hours."

"I'm all good." She shot him a quick glance before looking back at her work. "You don't have to stay. If you have somewhere to be."

"I have nowhere to be."

"You sure? No TV show you're desperate to binge-watch? No woman—or man—waiting for you back home?" She said it like a throwaway line but he could tell her gaze was no longer focused on the screen.

"No woman—or man—awaiting my return." He couldn't believe he was about to ask this. "Do you need to call anyone?"

"Me? No! *No.*"

"Will Zoe worry?"

"Zoe will not." She shot him a glance. "She'll be on the phone to Lance—the army boyfriend who is moving in any day now. Her place has very thin walls."

"Is your desire to stay here due to a desire to keep working or to give them space?"

"Both."

He had nothing to say to that. His entire reason for being in the country was a severe case of avoidance.

He picked up the phone, called down to the restaurant and discovered the chef was French. It was a few moments before he realised Evie was watching him, her fingers now still, her gaze on his mouth.

"*Oui*," he drawled, agreeing to the chef's suggestion. "*Et le poivron rouge, champignons, olives. D'accord.*"

When he rang off, he cleared his throat. "Dinner will be here in fifteen minutes. I should have asked if you have allergies."

She put the laptop onto the coffee table and stretched her arms and legs out in front of her. "I can eat anything. Except mushrooms and olives and red something. Peppers?"

Armand baulked. Until he saw the smile at the edge of her mouth. The muscles around his eyes tugged, creaking from under-use. "You speak French?"

"Not a jot. I'm just good at seeing patterns."

"Patterns?"

"Patterns—patterns everywhere. In sounds, in texture, in numbers, in code. I'm not sure why. Or how. My grandfather says I always lined up my jelly beans in coloured rows as a kid. And I took to knitting like a duck to water." She motioned to the knitted hat hanging on the hook on the wall by her desk. "My brain is simply wired that way. You?"

"Are you asking if I see patterns? Or how my brain is wired?"

"Whatever you'd like to share. We have fifteen minutes to fill, after all."

Armand moved deeper into the room. "What would you like to know?"

Evie's eyes never left his. "I'd built you up in my head as this strong, silent type. I had no idea it would be that easy!"

Armand stopped, crossed his arms.

"Fine. Okay. Here's a question: I get that your skills and knowledge are wide and varied, but what makes you the one Jonathon called in to do this job when you clearly know nothing about the kinds of technology that are his bread and butter?"

Trust her to cut straight to the quick. For the answer was complicated. A mass of thorny tangles and dark alleys and the kind of moments in a man's life only the very oldest of friends could understand. And forgive.

"We've known one another for a long time."

"Since university."

"How did you—?"

"His autobiography. I was rereading it last night and saw he studied Economics in France. I'm clever that way."

Armand scoffed. "You've read that schlock? More than once?"

Evie blinked. "As have you."

When he didn't respond she turned towards him, tucking one leg beneath her, leaning her elbow on the back of the couch, her head dipping into her palm. "On the train. A couple of weeks back. I think it's what gave me the impetus to look into career opportunities here when my last job went belly-up."

She'd watched him on the train. Just as he'd noticed her. Days ago. The knowledge settled, sliding into the dry cracks inside him like the first raindrops after a drought.

"Then you are my fault," he said.

"Completely." A grin spread slowly across her lovely face, like a sunrise in fast-forward. "Which explains how you know him but not why he came to you. Why he trusted you."

"Are you always this impertinent?"

"Are you always this obstructive?"

Armand breathed in. Breathed out. This woman.

He sank down onto the armrest of the couch. "My family—"

"The Debusseys of Paris," she said swishing a hand across the sky. His mother would like that. Would like her.

He tucked that thought away, nice and deep. "The very same. Despite the fact we have been in the business of art for generations—curation, auctioneering, patronising and owning—I did not go into the family business, instead joining the Légion Étrangère."

"The…strange legion… You were in the *French Foreign Legion*? Still waters, indeed." Her eyes ran over his suit, all the way down to his hand-made loafers and back up again. Then, "On *purpose*?"

This time as he smiled the muscles around his eyes tugged not quite so hard. As if they were warming up. "That's how it works."

A beat, then, "I might be mistaken, but I always had the sense it was a bit of a renegade unit, filled with murderers and thieves, men running from the law. Called on to intervene in the world's most dangerous hot spots at a moment's notice. While wearing berets."

"You are not far off. Any man may enlist, running from the law or otherwise. Bar those who've committed blood crimes and drug crimes."

She held up both hands, palms out. "I stand mistaken. Sounds like a lovely bunch of guys. You said any *man*…"

"No women."

She rolled her eyes. "Why am I not surprised?"

Armand went on to explain why. "The factors as to why are multiple: history; biological stamina. The men need to concentrate on the mission at hand, not concerning themselves with the safety of the women—"

But Evie held up a hand to stop him. "Spare me. And look around this place when you next get a chance. Tell me how many of the people working here are female and then explain to me what that has to do with biological stamina or the Safety of The Women."

*Touché.*

"So Armand Debussey of the art-loving Debusseys of Paris, how is it that you came to join this band of ne'er-do-wells?"

Till that moment the conversation had been light. Easy. For it was that time of night when the sky turned soft and voices gentled. Where words spilled readily as the last vestiges of daylight faded away. It was the time of night when soldiers had to be at their most diligent. When shadows could be men and men shadows.

"It's truly not that interesting."

She shifted, her hair spilling through her fingers, the light catching her cheekbones, her jaw, the curve of her lashes just so, her tone hushed as she said, "It is to me."

Armand felt the past creeping cold and slow up the back of his neck. For Lucia—his ex-wife— had felt the same. She'd fallen for the hero. Had never understood that at the end of a mission he didn't want to come home to a rent-a-crowd, to rehash the gritty details. Home for him was a place of quiet comfort, of warmth, clean sheets and locked doors.

When reality finally hit, she'd felt tricked. Perhaps even justifiably so. For he was very good at his job, his company growing exponentially in those early years, becoming the name in European private security and exposition of corporate espionage. But all the success in the world did not make up for the way dealing with the lowest of the low chipped away at a man's soul.

"If 'not interesting' means you don't want to talk about it, that's okay. Granddad fought in the Korean War and he needed to be in the right place, right moment, for the stories to come out." Evie shifted so he saw her in a new light—those rich brown eyes, the sweet curve of her smile, the insouciance of torn jeans, messy hair and slightly chipped black fingernails.

She was no Lucia. She was wholly herself.

Kind, hard-working, curious and genuine. No ulterior motives. No judgement.

Armand found himself saying, "Men come to the Legion for any number of reasons: travel, bloodlust, the desire to do good in the world, a second chance. There are seekers, there are hiders and there are the romantics. Only one in four makes it through the sit-down exam, medical, fitness, interview, psych test. Those who do are required to give up their nationality, and their name."

She sat forward, eyes wide, taking it all in.

"Training occurs for many months—in weapons, teamwork, standing still, marching through snow, following orders. Deserters are not uncommon. Those who make it emerge clear-eyed and well-shaven. Reborn. One."

"Mmm…" she said, her mouth twisting. "I can probably find everything you've just given me on their website. Tell me they didn't take one look at you and know they had something special."

"Turned out my family name was irrelevant."

"I wasn't talking about your name."

Armand's chest tightened. He breathed through it. Tried at least. It was becoming harder to steel himself against the onslaught that was Evie.

"Who I was didn't matter," he said, his voice coarse. "Only what I did from that moment on."

And within the ranks Armand found true *esprit de corps*—not based on where a person was from, who they knew, but how they conducted themselves.

He had learned faster, worked harder than anyone else and soon, despite the levelling nature of the corps, he had risen fast, his affinity with languages, with anthropological nuances, seeing him promoted swiftly, until he was put at the helm of a sharply honed team. A dagger hidden within the end of a blunt tool.

"Those men," she said, "the ones you brought in to help you find that little girl. Your Action Adventure All-Stars. That's how you knew them, isn't it? No better way to learn who you can trust than living in the trenches together."

"As much as it's possible to trust a bunch of ne'er-do-wells."

Evie shifted again, this time unhooking the band from her hair till it spilled into her hands. She gave her scalp a scratch and hummed with pleasure.

With no window to show if it was night or day—a trick used in department stores and torture chambers—Armand felt the quiet settling, the sense of possibility, of intimacy hovering on the air.

"Did you ever consider becoming a ne'er-do-well yourself?" Armand asked. "With your skill it would be a lucrative choice."

"Nah. I've always been a good girl." She batted her lashes, as if butter wouldn't melt in her mouth. "Preferring to build rather than tear down."

"An idealist. Like Jonathon. No wonder this is your dream job."

Her mouth twisted, her brow furrowing as she glanced towards the door. "Well, not exactly."

Armand stilled. "You told Jonathon otherwise."

She held up a finger. "I said this was *a* dream job, not my dream job."

"There's a difference?"

"When I was little, like four or five, my dream was to become a dairy farmer. My mum and I both grew up on my granddad's dairy farm, so it wasn't a huge leap. Then I turned eight, started taking the bus to school, and realised there were other jobs in the world. Bus driver! Teacher! When Granddad had heart problems I was determined to become a cardiologist."

When Armand frowned, she said, "He's good. Doing great. Clucked over like a prime rooster by a plethora of single septuagenarians in a very posh retirement village."

"And your mother?"

A shadow fell over her eyes, and she slouched a little in her seat. Always sunny—or bolshie, or impertinent, or frustrated—she was vibrant in every guise. Only now she seemed leeched of colour.

She said, "Not everyone *has* an all-consuming dream that sticks with them their entire life. My mother did."

The greyness swept over her, all the way to her fingertips as they began fidgeting with the ends of her short nails.

"What was it? Her dream?"

Her eyes lifted to his and he caught a flash, the glow inside her pulsing back to life. He felt the same pulse in himself, a beat of heat and light. His hand moved to his belly. To put a stop to it, or to hold it close. He couldn't be entirely sure.

"My mother was one of a kind. A true free spirit. She wanted to be an artist from the moment she held a crayon. She moved to Melbourne to follow her dream, only she never quite got a foothold. Then I came along and she went back to the farm. She died when I was six. Suddenly. Ruptured cerebral aneurysm."

She shot him a smile to say it was okay, it was a long time ago, but it was short. Flat. "My grand-dad did become a dairy farmer but it wasn't his big dream either. But he found immense pleasure in following his curiosity—getting his pilot's licence, inventing a board game, writing a book about colonial Australia. When I was born in the dead of winter he asked the Country Women's Association to teach him how to knit. In every baby photo I'm wearing a different beanie."

She breathed deep, sat taller.

"Where I'm from most local girls marry the local boys and keep local house while raising local babies. The only thing I liked about the local boys was how easily I could whip them gaming. With one hand tied behind my back. Literally. One day Granddad read that programming was the way of the future and cleared out a corner of the attic for a desk and a computer; he signed us up for Wi-Fi, signed me up for an online course in programming games and I was hooked."

"Follow your curiosity," Armand repeated, the feel of the words on his tongue new and fresh. For it was a concept he had never considered before. Raised to strive, to succeed, he had done just that, equating failure in any of his endeavours as failure in himself.

But to step back, to look inward, to know one-self enough to be comfortable with change—change of circumstance, change of heart, change of mind—with simply following one's curiosity; what a powerful, yet devastatingly simple, view.

"And now?" he asked. "If you were given the chance to follow your curiosity right now, what would you do?"

Something capricious flashed over her eyes; hints of humour, intrigue, and heat. A feeling he understood too well. For he had been wrestling with the same curiosity about her too. Fighting to keep it contained, hidden, lest it create discord, drama, dissension.

In that moment he paused, breathed, and simply let it be.

"You mean work-wise, right?" she asked.

A smile slid onto his face. "Of course."

"Other than ballerina princess firefighter astronaut?"

"You tell me."

Her mouth twisted as she tried to decipher if he really wanted to know, then eventually said, "I'd love to have a team of my own. Hand-picked. Enthusiastic. Creative. Nice. To develop the million game and app ideas I have mapped out in my "One Day" file. Game apps. Health apps. Learning apps. Much like our esteemed employer, actually. Have you ever had a job like that? That made you feel like you were contributing in a real, honest way?"

As she asked it Armand realised that, at one time, he had.

"Those first months after the foiled kidnap, when we started getting work without even looking for it, I had no choice but to organise, to create a framework, a business model. To hire in. It was wild. Crazy busy. But fulfilling. Yes."

Not just the work but also the knowledge he was giving good men secure futures went soul-deep. Allowing him to fall into bed at night with a sense of exhausted contentment for the first time in his life.

And yet his sense of duty had meant he'd allowed himself to be pulled away. Driven by the deep-seated need to do the right thing by all those he cared for. Not just his men. To keep his family safe and happy. Lucia safe and happy. Putting himself and his own needs last, as he'd always known deep down he was the strongest of them all.

No wonder the cracks had set in. No wonder he'd begun to feel lost in the fog. He'd buried his idiosyncratic spark, his *curiosity*, so deep below the layers of duty he'd forgotten how to recognise it at all.

"Were none of your Action Adventure All-Stars available to help you on this job?"

Armand's brow twitched. The thought of any of the brutes who worked for him knowing how to turn on a computer, much less understand how one worked, was laughable. Besides, it had been many months since he'd handed over the day-to-day running of his company to his second in command, knowing the man would not bother him unless civilisation was on the brink of collapse.

"It's a one-man job."

Evie's eyebrow crept higher and higher.

"Apologies; one man and one woman."

A knock came at the door.

Evie and Armand's gazes caught. Evie bit back a smile and Armand laughed, his voice raw, as he ran a hand up the back of his neck. "More shadows than you'd bargained for going down that path?"

She shook her head. "I've never been afraid of the dark."

"Well, you should be."

All he got for his efforts was a hint of a smile,

glinting dark eyes and a sense of unfurling heat deep within. Volcanic. Untapped. Vast.

He drew himself off the armrest and moved to the door. He gathered the pizzas and wine and put them on the coffee table, watching as Evie slowly lowered herself to her knees, then onto her backside on the floor. Her long legs tucked under her.

"Pizza and *wine*?" she asked.

Armand smiled. "Of course wine—I am French."

She held out a glass. "*Vive la France.*"

They ate and drank in companionable silence. The room warm, the light golden. The curl of interest and attraction simmering between them.

When Armand offered Evie the last piece she didn't argue, taking it with a happy sigh.

After which they cleaned up and went back to their respective corners, Evie with her profile lit blue by the computer screen, Armand taking a break from the real world within the pages of a novel. Or pretending at the very least.

"Armand," said Evie a little while later.

"Yes, Evie."

"When you ran to the Legion, what kind of recruit were you? The seeker? The hider? Or the romantic?" The pause between her second guess and her third was infinitesimal. And thoroughly telling.

"Wasn't there something about a thorn, or a knot, that required your attention?"

She looked over at him. "There was. And you really don't have to stay. I'm a big girl. Tough as nails. No dew in these eyes."

"I'll stay till you're ready to leave."

"Because we've not been in the trenches long enough for you to trust me not to make off with all this fancy equipment?"

"Because we are in this together. A team. No man—or woman—left behind."

Her gaze widened a fraction—dewy as all get-out.

Her voice was a little rough as she said, "Okay, then."

Watching her settle into her chair, hooking a foot up onto the seat and resting her chin on her knee, all coltish and clever and keen, he no longer even trusted himself.

# CHAPTER SEVEN

EVIE FOUND AN error in the code. Not a virus, or a time bomb—and no evidence of sabotage—just a thread that could have been better written.

She was disappointed that it hadn't been incendiary. But also pretty impressed with the fact it was the first error she'd found. Seriously sophisticated coding. Which made sense, as Jonathon was far too savvy to put his name on anything less.

She fixed the problem, then left her own trail back in case she needed to show it to Jonathon later on.

She stretched her arms over her head and rocked her neck from side to side. Her brain thus no longer locked onto her work, Armand's last words found a nick and slid back into her mind.

*Because we are in this together. A team. No man—or woman—left behind.*

The fact she'd been able to concentrate at all after that little bombshell had been a small miracle. Her mother had passed away when she was six. She'd never met her father. Her granddad had practically kicked her out of home—after the local doctor had convinced him it was far better for him to be in a residential village, surrounded by his peers and medical help, than stuck on the farm with a bad heart. And now Zoe was moving into the next phase of her life.

She knew her granddad was in good hands where he was, which was why she was happy to pay extra for the rent. And she was delighted for Zoe and Lance. Didn't mean she didn't ache for the fact that everything was changing.

No, Evie was not new to the concept of being left behind.

And yet Armand had stayed. It was a little thing in comparison. Keeping her company for no other reason than he believed it was the right thing to do. She understood that when the job was done he'd go back to the far more exciting life he'd led before. Yet the man was making it terribly difficult to remember why she shouldn't be falling for him in a big way.

Once the first yawn hit, Evie knew she was done. She glanced at her phone to find it was nearing midnight. The witching hour. When shadows and noises and illicit thoughts sprang up where in daylight they would not. She found herself actually looking forward to falling into her futon, lumpy and less than private though it was.

She saved her work and set her own secret encryption protocols in place. Better safe than sorry.

Evie clumped heavily over to Armand's desk.

"Done?" he asked, looking up from his book.

"For now," she said, her voice husky from under-use. "My eyes are crossing and my fingers feel twice their normal size. Skiving off?"

"Skiving?"

"Playing truant. Cutting class. Instead of working, you're reading…"

She leaned further over his desk, tipped the cover towards her. And nearly fell over when she saw the title.

Armand noticed. He noticed everything. Now she knew he'd been in the French Foreign Legion of all things she had an inkling as to why.

If she wasn't great at reading people, she got her heart stomped on. If he wasn't great at reading people, people died.

He turned the book over to glance at the cover. Hardback, ivy scrolled over the borders. The title: *The Poetry of Elizabeth Browning*.

"Not a fan of Browning?" he asked.

"Hmm?" Evie squeaked, thinking, *Poetry, poetry, poetry…*

"Elizabeth Barrett Browning."

"Um… I'm not sure I know anything she wrote." *Think, Evie, think. Change the subject.*

*How 'bout them Cubs?* usually worked. But what did they even play? Baseball? Football? Lacrosse?

"I doubt that," he said.

She watched in growing horror as Armand flicked a few pages, pressed the open book to the table. In his deep, rough, lilting voice he read:

*How do I love thee? Let me count the ways.*
*I love thee to the depth and breadth and height*
*My soul can reach, when feeling out of sight*
*For the ends of being and ideal grace.*
*I love thee to the level of every day's*
*Most quiet need, by sun and candle-light.*
*I love thee freely, as men strive for right.*

"Oh," Evie managed through the pulse beating hard and fast in her throat. "*That* Elizabeth Barrett Browning. Sure, she's great."

*It's just a book*, her subconscious said. *The fact he's reading poetry doesn't mean anything. Heaps of guys read poetry. Educated French guys from pre-eminent artistic families, anyway. Now, say goodnight and go home.*

"Then you do like poetry," she said.

*Really? Are you trying to humiliate yourself?*

"Some. I speak several languages but I read them far less. While here I thought it best to brush up on my English vocabulary. Poetry, newspapers, literature, websites. It all helps."

"Cool."

*The man's reading Browning in a language that is not his own and all you can come up with is "Cool"?*

"Have you ever written poetry?" she asked. And her subconscious threw up its hands and left.

"Why do I feel as if we've covered this already?"

"We haven't," she insisted. "Not really. Have you ever written poetry?"

He pushed back his chair and collected his things. "Of course."

*Of course!* French, gorgeous, grouchy and an avid reader. How silly of her to even question him!

"Are you ready to go?" he asked.

And it took Evie a moment to realise he'd let her off the hook on which she'd been floundering. "Hmm? Yes. *Yes.* I'm done. All done."

Armand held out a hand towards the door, and Evie scooted by, holding her breath so as not to catch the scent of him—warm, elegant, inviting.

Downstairs, the Bullpen was like a sleeping giant: the hum of machines, the low lights, as if a good kick and it would rear back to comic-bright life in a second.

They hit the alley and walked side by side through the near-darkness, moonlight slanting over the artwork decorating the brickwork and over the angles of Armand's face. Their shoes making music against the cobblestones beneath their feet.

If they hurried they'd still make the last train. If they didn't hurry she could still call a cab and she'd get to enjoy the strange magic of walking with this man in the moonlight. Tuck it away like a little gift to bring out and admire as she lay on her lonely futon wherever she ended up.

"I have organised a car," said Armand.

And Evie realised they'd hit the street. A sleek black car with tinted windows rumbled to life against the kerb. She could just make out the out-line of a driver in a peaked hat. "You take it. I live an easy walk from the station."

"Nevertheless." Armand opened the rear door for her.

The street lamps dropped perfect circles of golden light on the footpath, a light breeze rustled the branches of a sapling planted in a hole in the concrete. And Evie found she couldn't move.

She felt as if she had to say something—more than a simple thank-you for the car. They'd made a kind of breakthrough tonight. She wouldn't say they were friends. More like interested observers. Visitors at the zoo, only neither could be sure which of them was the exhibit.

He watched her watching him—quietly, patiently. As if he too knew what it meant to require time to figure things out.

What if he had written her the poem? What if he'd been waiting for her to figure it out all along? But she couldn't ask. It would have been embarrassing a few days ago, but now—yes or no—it would change everything.

And yet the possibility snagged at something inside her. Some place warm and soft and fragile. For the crush she'd hoped would dissolve away the more she got to know him had instead evolved as she'd come to regard him with respect, with intrigue, with a yearning that never quite went away.

If it was him she *had* to let him down. To break the fortune cookie's curse.

He was tougher than he seemed. Seriously

tough, she'd come to realise. Warrior-, hero-, soldier-level tough. He'd get over it.

The real question was: would she?

The breeze kicked up, lifting the hair not tucked into her beanie. She pushed it behind her ear.

Somewhere a clock struck, the chimes counting down to midnight.

As if a finger had been hooked into her shirt she felt herself sway away from the car. Towards Armand.

He noticed. He always noticed. Meaning he probably knew all about the crush. The intrigue. The respect. The yearning.

His hand tightened on the top of the door. Yeah, he knew.

His feet stayed where they were, moonlight shining off his nut-brown dress shoes. "Get in the car, Evie."

"In a minute."

When she took another step closer his nostrils flared but he still didn't move. The man was a rock.

And the way her life was floundering, maybe a rock was exactly what she needed. In the interim. Until she was back on solid ground.

Armand looked off to the side, his eyes full of shadows, the breeze sending waves through his hair. After a long, slow out-breath his gaze came back to hers.

The figurative finger hooked into her shirt gave another little yank and she stumbled forward one more step. "I wanted to thank you. For tonight. For sticking around and letting me do what I needed to do. For making me feel like part of a team."

A muscle twitched in his jaw.

The wind caught her hair again, catching in her eyelashes, on her lip. When she tugged it free, Armand's gaze dropped to her mouth. And stayed there.

"Whatever it takes to get the job done." His voice was deep, a rumble that shot through her body before zapping into the earth beneath her feet.

"See, that's exactly how I feel."

Yet her heart slammed against her ribs as if it was trying to break free. How could it not when he gazed at her lips as if haunted by the space between them? When he looked at her as if she was not only a curiosity, but also a disruption? As if he was confounded by the very fact of her?

The fortune cookie bobbed up in the corner of her mind like a final-warning sign. Danger Ahead! Though it was a bogus excuse. Or a case of apophenia. Sufferers looked for patterns in random data to make sense of the world. She'd looked it up. It had first been discovered during schizophrenia research. Good to know.

As she stood there in the moonlight, the breeze tugging at her hair, her clothes, with Armand clearly holding on so tight, she knew—if she believed in patterns as much as she claimed to, then ignoring them when it came to Armand was hypocritical.

She wasn't alone in this. She wasn't alone.

Before she could stop herself, Evie took a single step forward and pressed her lips against Armand's.

No other part of them touched. He still held on to the car door, her back foot resting toe down on the ground.

It was delicate, daring, and it took less than a second to know she'd stepped over a line.

But she didn't move. Couldn't. Her mouth remained gentle against his. Cool to warm. Dewy to dry. Her entire body alight with the most exquisite sensation she'd ever known.

*Kiss me back*, she thought. *Or push me away. Stop time. Rewind.* Anything but the beautiful agony of the in-between.

Then, just as the backs of Evie's eyes began

to burn, Armand's slowly closed. His hand slid around her back. He pulled her into the hard length of his body and a fist of tightly held desire unfurled inside her.

Weighted, heavy, her eyelids lowered and she grabbed a hunk of his shirt as she tilted and pressed her lips more fully to his. Testing, tasting, drowning in release. The warmth of his mouth, his body, a stark contrast to the wintry breeze at her back.

His other hand sank into her hair, his thumb brushing her cheek, her ear, dislodging her beanie, before he nudged her lips apart and set her world on fire.

Her hands were running up his back, sliding through his hair, over his spectacular backside, her knee nudging between his until every part of her that could lean into every part of him did.

Minutes, hours, aeons—probably seconds— later Armand pulled back, tipping his forehead to hers. Bodies heaving, they found their breath.

Evie felt less as though she'd been kissed than as if she'd been hit by a train. She couldn't feel her feet and her vision spun with stars. She still gripped a fistful of his shirt but no way was she ready to let go. It was the only thing keeping her from sinking into a puddle at his feet.

A car horn beeped long and hard, young male voices whooping and laughing as their car cruised by.

Evie came back into her own body enough to press back and look into Armand's eyes.

After one more deep breath Armand looked up, his stormy gaze tangling with hers.

What she saw there brought her back to earth with a thud.

For the man was in pain. She could see it in the curve of his shoulders. In the furrow of his brow. In the tempest of emotion in his eyes.

While she felt wracked with lust, Armand looked as though someone had just discovered the bruise in the centre of his soul and jabbed it with a sharp stick.

It was too much.

He was too much.

What had she done?

Before he could say a word she yanked open the car door, leapt inside and gave the driver Zoe's address.

As the car eased smoothly out into the street Evie sank her face into her hands and screamed. Silently.

She'd *kissed* him. And he'd clearly wished she hadn't.

How the hell was she meant to face him again? At work? On the train? Every day? How was she meant to face herself? When acting contrary to her own interests over a man was the one thing she'd been determined she'd never do?

As the train neared Armand's usual pick-up spot the next morning Evie's leg jiggled so hard it was making her travel-sick.

"How much coffee did you drink this morning?" Zoe asked.

"One, two cups." Evie literally couldn't remember. "I didn't sleep well."

"Bad dreams?"

"Not exactly."

"Ah, I see." Zoe nudged her in the shoulder. "*Bad* dreams. I bet I know who's the leading man. And speaking of dreamy, look who it is."

Evie knew exactly who Zoe was talking about and kept her gaze trained determinedly on the window. If she didn't make eye contact perhaps he'd head to his old seat. And they could pretend the night before had never happened.

When she heard the pop of Zoe's phone taking a photo, her head snapped around. "What are you doing?"

Zoe showed her the picture and, yep, it was

Armand. "Seriously. That man is the very definition of a long, cool drink of water."

Knowing it was a losing battle, Evie glanced up from the phone to find Armand making his way through the carriage towards her. Her insides came over all gooey at the sight of him. He looked so French in his dark suit, dark shirt, dark tie, stubble now hitting sexy-beard length.

When she remembered how it felt to kiss him—the soft scrape of his stubble, the heat of his lips, Evie struggled to remember how to breathe.

Zoe said, "Lucky he's not completely to my taste, or I'd be in big trouble. I like rogues. Bad boys. And my daring Lance is the baddest of them all."

Evie thought back to Armand's revelations of his past adventures and decided not to tell Zoe lest she implode on the spot.

"Love poem or not, you are a fool if you don't at least put your hat in the ring there. Let me be your go-between. A fairy godmother if you will."

"Not necessary."

By the time Armand made it to their seat, Evie's leg was cramping from shaking so much.

This was for the best. Get the mortification over and done with. When his gaze connected with hers she braced herself... Only to melt from the head down.

"Good morning," he said in that voice of his, his gaze locked on to hers.

"Good morning!" Zoe sing-songed before Evie was able to find her voice.

"Sleep well?" he asked.

"Our Evie had bad dreams," Zoe said, helpfully. "Or were they good?"

"Not important," Evie said, her voice raw.

She could have sworn she saw a flicker of light behind the clouds in Armand's eyes. But the vision of him looking so pained the night before wiped it out.

Then Armand said, "I believe this is yours." He held out her beanie. The one that had fallen off her head when he'd kissed her.

Strike that. She'd kissed him. With the excuse she was trying to discover if he was the poet or the one the fortune cookie had told of. The truth was, she'd wanted to kiss him. So badly. Consequences be damned.

"Thanks." Evie leaned past Zoe and took the beanie, shoving it into her backpack.

She caught Zoe's eye when she sat up, to find her oldest friend watching her with far too much understanding on her face.

"So tell me about yourself, Armand. Married? Single? Got your eye on someone?"

Evie shot Zoe a death stare but her friend refused to engage, too busy was she keeping an eye on Armand to test his reaction. Little did Zoe know that the man was a Zen master.

Glancing at Armand as briefly as humanly possible, Evie said, "Ignore her. She's of the mistaken impression that anyone but her would care about such things."

When Zoe went to say something else, Evie leapt in. "Please leave him out of this. He already thinks Australians are too uptight about romance."

"Does he, now?"

"He's French. It came up."

"Hmm, he could be right," Zoe said. "Evie is being very circumspect about the prospects at work. Perhaps you can illuminate me."

"Zoe!" Evie wished she could climb under the train seats, despite whatever disgusting things lurked down there.

Then Armand said, "What about your young friend in the Bullpen? The one who always wears a cap."

Evie's jiggling leg came to a grinding halt. Was he seriously suggesting what she thought he was suggesting? And after he'd held her to him the way he had the night before, kissing her until her knees no longer worked?

"You mean Jamie?" Evie offered helpfully. "I do not want Jamie." Then something made her add, "But even if I did *want him*, I still have no intention of mixing work and play."

"Ah, you're still stuck on that, then."

Evie's leg started up again, now at double speed. "Not *stuck*. That makes it sound as if it's not my decision. I am completely determined."

"If you say so."

The train began to slow, the metal beneath the belly of the beast screeching as they came to a halt. Evie ducked under the strap of her cross-body bag and stood, stepping over the school bags at her feet, and over Zoe's knees.

Till she found herself behind Armand. She could smell his aftershave. Or maybe it was just him. She closed her eyes and breathed. Earthy, clean and delicious.

When she opened her eyes he'd moved away, heading towards the doors.

"Off you go, then," Zoe said. "Can't wait to hear what 'comes up' today."

Once she could no longer see him, Evie made a dash for the door, catching it just in time. Her beanie slipped sideways, one of the puppy-dog ears dipping into her eye. She fixed it then took off at lightning speed towards the office so as not to be late.

"Evie!" It was Armand.

Of course, he wanted to walk with her today. Right when she felt all strange and discombobulated, confused and raw.

"Evie, please wait."

Evie stopped and spun, only Armand hadn't seen it coming and barrelled into her.

He grabbed her by the upper arms, turning her, their legs entwining, the world going topsy-turvy until he found balance enough for the both of them. There they stood, breath intermingling, bodies slammed against one another as gravity and momentum settled back to a normal ratio.

"Look at me," he insisted.

"I'd rather not."

"Why? Are you afraid you'll kiss me again?"

Evie laughed, the sound only slightly hysterical. "Don't panic. I got your message. I won't be doing that again."

"Evie."

She flinched at the intensity in his voice, the way it rolled over her skin like a caress. And she couldn't help it. Her eyes found his.

"I'm sorry," she said.

"You have nothing to apologise for."

Evie rolled her eyes. Or at least she tried to. With Armand so close—close enough she could see the flecks of navy in his irises, could trace the shape of his jaw beneath his stubble—she was struggling to maintain control of herself.

Her voice was raw as she said, "I saw the look on your face last night, Armand. You don't need to throw Jamie in my face as a way to try to deal with me."

A muscle beneath his eye twitched. "He seems like a nice young man."

Evie laughed again. "You've barely said two words to the guy, so how would you know if he's a nice young man?"

Armand breathed out long and slow. "You're right. Most people blur into one another in the end. A rare few have surprised me. Of which you are most definitely one."

Evie felt herself flush all over at the look in Armand's eyes, the rough note in his voice.

Then he let go of her with one hand to tug her beanie into place. "Jamie is off the table. You would never find contentment with a man of his ilk. You need someone who knows your worth."

Now what was he saying? That *he* was that

man? No, there was still that sense of a bruise about him. As though if she looked beneath the sharp suit she'd find he'd been beaten black and blue.

She glanced between his eyes but found him as barricaded as ever. The colour in his eyes so dark she could no longer differentiate the blues from the greys.

And yet he still held her. Close. So close she couldn't stop trembling.

That line she'd stepped over the night before? In that moment she knew—there was no going back. Not for her.

"What if I'm not looking for contentment?" she asked.

Her conscience perked up. *That's* exactly *what you're looking for, kiddo. Keeping your dreams manageable, your expectations reasonable. No running back to the farm for you!*

"Evie…"

"You kissed me too, you know. Sure, I kissed you first, but you kissed me back. And it was a good kiss."

His eyebrow lifted in the international sign of, *Come on. It was better than good.*

"Fine. It was a great kiss." She'd still been floating three inches off the ground when she'd slunk into Zoe's apartment forty minutes later. "And yet it can't happen again."

*Why not?* she asked herself. But then he got that look in his eye again. As if kissing him was a death sentence.

"What do we do about it?" she asked.

"Why can't we do nothing?"

"Nothing." *Huh.*

"The moon was high," he said. "The hour was late. The wine was good. The work intense. And we kissed. Not everything in life has a deeper meaning."

Evie reared back. "When you were in the jungle with your men, and it was late, and you hadn't seen another soul in hours, and things were about as intense as things can ever get, did that kind of thing happen to you a lot?"

Evie stilled, imagining his next step would be to throw his hands up and pace away from her, railing at the gods in French.

Instead he threw back his head and laughed.

It was a hell of a thing. Rich, rough and sexy as hell. It was also more unexpected than the flinch. Because he'd let himself go. The containment field that protected him gone, leaving her feeling heady, weak, as if the bottom had dropped out of her life.

"Maybe this is a huge joke to you," Evie said, "but it wasn't to me. I don't just go around kissing random people."

*Random. Good one. Make it sound as if you haven't been crushing on him for weeks.*

"And," she continued, "while I'd put money on the fact that you are perfectly happy to slink back into your metaphorical cave, I'm not. I don't run from my mistakes—I face up to them."

The laughter slowly fled from his eyes as a new kind of darkness followed in its wake. Not a scary darkness, oh, no. The kind of darkness that sucked you in and tumbled you about and you didn't mind a single bit.

"You believe it was a mistake?" Armand asked, his voice deep and rough and devastating.

"Isn't that what *you* just said?"

Armand watched her with that darkly quiet way he had about him. She felt giddy, as if the spinning hadn't quite come to a stop. And the look in his eyes, those dark, stormy, intense, beautiful, warm, engaging eyes—

Then someone bumped them. And another person.

Another train had pulled in, the early-morning commuters swarming over the platform like water bursting from a dam. Jostling them apart.

His fingers curled away from her arms, the skin left behind turning cold, the nerves sharp.

And, seeing daylight, she turned and hustled towards work. And this time he didn't try to stop her.

# CHAPTER EIGHT

EVIE KEPT HER head down as she barrelled through the Bullpen so as not to get stuck chatting games or algorithms with any of the boys.

And they were boys. Boys who lived on pizza and hamburgers, who she knew would live in places any right-minded landlord would condemn.

Growing up with her granddad and his friends, she'd known men who could roof a house, cook a decent meal and talk about everything from historical Russian literature to modern-day Russian politics.

She hadn't realised how much she'd missed being around actual grown-ups until she'd met Armand. For he was serious. Experienced. Despite his stubborn determination not to enter the electronic age he was the most intelligent man she had ever met.

And there was no running away from the fact her feelings for Armand had well and truly tipped from playful crush to "it's complicated".

So much for not dating fellow employees. Not that they were dating. Ha! They could barely hold a civil conversation without disagreement or culture clash or retreating to their own corners to lick their wounds. Or holding one another. Looking deep into each other's eyes. Kissing.

Evie was up the stairs and halfway down the hall when she pulled up to a dead stop.

There was only one thing for it. She *had* to ask to be put onto another project. For she couldn't lose this job. Working for Jonathon Montrose was the pinnacle—being fired by Jonathon Montrose a career death knell. If it ever came to that she may as well hang up her shingle and go home.

She'd kept the farm after all—renting it out to cover rates repairs and not much more—in case her granddad ever wanted to return.

In that moment she realised how desperately she wanted to stay. This city had got under her skin. She wanted this. Melbourne was her dream. She was not a farm girl any more; she was already *home*.

She paced back to Jonathon's door, raised her hand to knock. Stopped herself just in time.

He'd ask why. What could she possibly say? The truth? Her eyes slammed shut and she let out a sob.

"Evie?"

Evie flinched and opened her eyes to find Jonathon standing beside her, coffee mug in hand, Imogen peeling off to her office.

"Hi, Mr Montrose. Good morning."

"Did you want to see me? Everything okay?"

*No. Everything's not okay. The man you've lumped me with is like a dormant volcano and I can't be sure if I'm in lust with him or so burnt by my last twisted working relationship I'm building castles in the sky.*

"Everything's great!"

"Glad to hear it. How's the project coming along? Any chance it'll be wrapped up soon?"

Evie thought of the knot she'd tripped over in the programming the night before. The one that had had her staying late in the first place. Until the little carpet picnic with Armand had scrambled her brain.

"I'm getting close. I can smell it."

"Just you?"

"I mean we. We're getting close."

*Real close. His lips touched mine and I saw stars.*

"Close to finding the problem, I mean."

Her boss's eyes narrowed, though she could have sworn his mouth twitched with a smile. "Excellent. And the other things we spoke about?"

Despite the fact she wasn't feeling all that delighted with the man right now, she still wasn't about to turn on him with Jonathon.

"I can handle him." Evie backed away, then turned on her heel and fled.

Thankful her thumbprint now opened the lock on the first try, she ducked inside and shut the door.

After inhaling a few deep breaths she darted over to her desk, dumped her backpack, hung up her beanie and opened up the program, determined to have good news for Jonathon soon. For the sooner this project was over and done with, the sooner she and Armand would no longer be stuck in a tiny room together. She'd have hopefully impressed Jonathon enough to keep her on. And Armand could get on with his life of international intrigue.

Armand arrived on cue. He lurked darkly in the doorway. All scruffy hair and intense energy.

Evie turned up the music in her headphones and got scrolling, still hyperaware of the man as he dropped his briefcase to the floor with a thud, picked up the phone and proceeded to bark down the line in French.

She didn't bother trying to translate. Instead she did what she should have been doing the whole time and got to work.

She managed another minute and a half before Jonathon's voice suddenly filled the room. "Evie. Armand."

"Jeez!" Evie cried, tearing off her headphones, gaze darting about the room. "What the heck was that?"

Armand glanced at his phone, pressed a button that had lit up red and said, "Is this the great and powerful Oz?"

A beat went by before the disembodied voice once more boomed into the room. "You know damn well who this is, funny guy. You both need to clear your schedules tomorrow evening. Cancel plans. Postpone any dates."

Evie couldn't help herself. She glanced towards Armand, only to find him determinedly not looking her way.

"Anyone with eyes can see that the two of you are still butting heads."

*Well, that was one way to put it.*

"You two need to find a way to be in the same room together without it ending in tears."

Oh, God, was that what he thought? "Jonathon, we're getting along just great. At the very least, Armand has never made me cry."

Then she looked to Armand, who was staring

at his desk as if trying to burn a hole in the top. She whispered, "Have I made *you* cry?"

Armand finally lifted his gaze to collide with hers. His eyes filled with humour and regret. Heat and sorrow. She wasn't sure what she wanted to do first—hug him or kiss him. Probably easiest to simply do both.

Jonathon went on. "I've organised a team-building exercise."

Evie's gaze shot to the phone as her entire body clenched in response. Not the horror of a grown-up "truth or dare" session. Or "two true things, one false thing". And the trust fall? The thought of having to fall into Armand's waiting arms in front of people was too disturbing for words.

"You can both wipe the grimaces from your faces," said the voice.

Evie looked frantically around her, searching for hidden cameras. She'd been there, after all.

"Jonathon—" Armand began.

But Jonathon had the luxury of not being in the room and cut him off. "Imogen has sent you both the details. I look forward to hearing your effusive thanks next week."

Armand's finger slowly lifted from the phone. It was moments before his gaze finally lifted to connect with hers.

"We don't really have to do this, do we?" Evie asked.

"I have found in life that we don't *have* to do anything. Only that which we feel we should. Or that which we truly want."

Evie swallowed, heat curling in her belly like a creeping vine in fast motion. No two guesses as to why she'd kissed Armand. Though she couldn't be certain as to why he'd kissed her back.

Either way, now that she'd promised Jonathon they were close—close to finding the answer, that was—her position at Game Plan felt more precarious than ever.

"Maybe he has a point," said Evie. "Maybe if we got to know each other more we could make more efficient use of our time."

Even in the low light she could see Armand's eyes narrow. Was he agreeing? Or was he imagining the same ways of "using their time" she was?

Evie broke eye contact by grabbing her phone. She scrolled through her mail till she found the team-building details. "There's just an address. A time. And a dress code: comfortable for freedom of movement."

No matter what Armand said, it was hardly as if she had a choice.

"I'm in if you are," she said, wondering if everything she said from now on would feel like a double entendre.

Armand said, "So be it."

At six o'clock the next evening, Armand found himself standing outside a corrugated iron door covered in graffiti reading "Escape Room Challenge".

"Is this what I think it is?" he asked, not bothering to disguise the lack of enthusiasm towards the endeavour.

Evie's big, dark eyes roved frenetically over the list of rules posted beside the door: *No one with heart conditions... No pregnant women... No children under sixteen years..."*

This vision of energy and light had kissed him.

And he'd kissed her. He could still taste her on his lips, feel the way she had sunk into his body. Her body soft and pliable. Completely trusting.

He should have put a stop to it then. Knowing that their attraction couldn't go anywhere. He'd seen too much darkness. Was bitter. Brittle. While Evie was endearing, charming, lovely from the inside out.

His time in Melbourne had been restorative. As if the smaller cracks were beginning to smooth over. Much of that was thanks to her. But some scars went so deep they leeched colour from a man's soul.

He'd meant it when he'd told her to find someone who knew her worth. But that person was not him. Could not be him. He struggled to reconcile with the regrets of his past. He'd never forgive himself if anything happened to her.

"What the heck was Jonathon thinking?" she asked.

"I often wonder the same thing."

"You do realise he's merely moved us about to go from one small room to another." Her hands moved to her hips, stretching the words "All My Friends Are Dead" over the dinosaur on her T-shirt tight across her curves. "Only this time we'll be locked in."

Evie looked up at him and he wondered if he looked as deeply put out as she did. But then she blinked, twice, and burst out laughing. The sound like birdsong. Like spring time.

He felt a kick at the corner of his mouth. Then another behind his ribs. Within a heartbeat he found himself back there again, deep in the memory of her kiss.

The surprise as her lips pressed against his—cool and soft. Then realisation that it was no surprise at all. Inevitable as the sunrise. Inescapable as breath.

Then her hand curling into his shirt, her knuckles sliding down his chest. Until he'd felt like bottled lightning.

After spending the past year of his life doing everything in his power not to feel anything at all he'd been unprepared, his neglected instincts reacting incongruously to his wishes, giving in wholly to sensation instead of dashing for cover.

A green light lit up over a door a couple of metres down the hall. It opened with a click and out sauntered Jamie, followed by three of his ilk.

Before he even knew he'd moved, Armand's fingers curled into his palms, his feet shifting into position as if he had an enemy in his sights.

As the kid squinted despondently into the brightness, wiping sweat from his brow, Armand told himself to stand the hell down.

"Jamie?" Evie called.

When Jamie saw that they had an audience, he rallied admirably. Squaring himself, finding a grin. "Why, hello, old man. Evie, love."

He sauntered up and slapped Armand on the back, hard enough to rock another man off his heels. But Armand was not any other man. He dropped a shoulder at the last second, leaving

Jamie wincing and rubbing at his hand. It felt rather good.

Then the guy leaned over to kiss Evie on the cheek.

And Armand could have taken him down. A single jab to the throat with a sharp hand ought to do it. A crack to the jaw with a closed fist if he felt like going old-school. Of course, a knee to the balls was foolproof.

"How was it?" Evie asked.

"Brilliant," Jamie said, as his cohorts muttered things along the lines of "impossible".

"First time?" Evie asked.

Jamie answered, "I've done VR versions, of course. But in the flesh? Never."

Armand scoffed.

"Problem?" Jamie asked.

"VR," he muttered. "What a cop-out."

There were gasps all around. Evie moved in closer, as if about to dive in front of him if the others attacked. Him. A man who could have the lot of them unconscious in seconds if he saw fit.

A strange sensation came over him. Warmth sliding through his insides as if he'd eaten hot soup too fast. He protected his own. It wasn't often anyone thought to stand up for him. Or feed him. Or make sure he was okay.

Jamie said, "Wait till you get in there. You know it is not real, but it feels real. Gives you a great glimpse into how you react in a crisis."

The kid poked a finger towards Armand's chest and it took everything he had not to grab the kid's fingers and twist.

"Jamie," Evie said, sliding a hand into Armand's elbow, "Armand has a better handle on that kind of thing than you realise."

She glanced at Armand, looking for permission. His shrug was as good as.

"He was in the French Foreign Legion."

"Whoa," said a cohort. "You for real?"

"For real," Armand deadpanned.

"Actual on-the-ground stuff?"

Armand nodded.

The cohorts oohed and ahhed. Said, "Man, that's cool."

While Jamie crossed his arms. "Sitting behind a desk pushing papers all day must feel like quite the departure."

"A combatant is a combatant," said Armand, eyes on Jamie.

Evie squeezed his arm. He looked down to find her face impassive. Then the edge of her mouth curved. Heat slid through him, only this time, like after jumping into a hot shower on a cold winter's day, it ached.

Before he had the chance to unpack all that that might mean, the light above their door began to flash yellow, which—according to the rules— meant they had a minute to enter before the game began.

Evie gave him a tug. "Come on, then, partner. I'm a genius. You're...you. Let's show these monkeys how this is really done."

For reasons he could feel guilty about later, Armand tucked a hand over hers and pulled her closer, smiling down at her and shooting Jamie and his friends an even bigger smile before opening the door to the Escape Room and closing it behind them.

It was dark, the lack of eyesight heightening his other senses. A sensation not new for him after his military training and years of organised insurrection.

Evie's skills were to be found in other areas, so she turned and walked right into him.

He grabbed her by the shoulders. Steadied her. Breathed in the cherry scent of her hair. Sweet and ingenuous. Like her.

So much for "getting to know one another".

Their awareness had ratcheted up to eleven, making the air crackle and the walls close in.

"Sorry," Evie breathed, her voice giving away the fact she was in the same state as he was. "I didn't expect it to be this dark."

"I believe that's the point."

Static crackled though a speaker and a TV flickered to life. Armand let Evie go and they both turned to watch a "news report" that set up the puzzle they had to work out. The name of their room was "Corporate Chaos" in which a thief embezzled from the International Monetary Fund, leaving the world broke and leading to World War III.

Images of the Wall Street stock market cut to shots of shredders and people crying and finally to men and women in combat gear climbing over the smoking rubble of a fallen city.

He was going to kill Jonathon. Using his bare hands. Nice and slow.

"You don't have PTSD, do you?" Evie asked.

His experiences in the Legion had never been an issue. The parameters were clear—make a plan, follow the plan, stay alive. It was the civilised world he'd struggled with. The tug of duty, the lure of freedom, the ache of disappointment. And the mind-bending pain of loss.

"No," Armand assured her. "Do you?"

"You're hilarious," she deadpanned.

And Armand felt himself smile.

Even in the deep darkness, the room lit only by the static now playing on the screen and a small green exit sign over the door, he saw Evie's gaze drop to his mouth and stay.

The room suddenly felt smaller. Warmer. Little shocks tingled across his skin. He felt like a teen, stuck in a closet playing Five Minutes in Heaven.

Only they were grown-ups. In a locked room. On their own. And they had half an hour.

"What do you reckon, soldier boy? Shall we do this?"

For a second, he imagined she'd read his mind.

Then she turned about, looking up and down and all around. "What do we need first? A key? A clue? A code?"

"Light," said Armand, watching the very same play over Evie's hair, the curve of her shoulders, the sweet planes of her lovely face. "What we need is light."

"That was amazing!"

Evie spun around, arms out to the side, revelling in the feel of the air-conditioning on her hot skin as they burst from the Escape Room twelve minutes and eighteen seconds after they'd entered.

For it had been ridiculously fun. Intense—for sure. Especially considering the size of the room—they couldn't move without brushing up against one another. Leaving Evie hot and flushed and wired. But the thrill of the game had taken them over, and once they'd found their beat it had been like a dance.

Armand had a labyrinthine mind, clever and flexible, twisting and turning and unravelling the trickiest clues with frightening speed. Leaving Evie to do her thing, to follow the breadcrumbs which stood out to her like fireflies in the dark.

She stopped spinning, wiped her damp hair off her face and faced Armand.

While she felt as if her T-shirt was sticking to her back, he looked as if he'd stepped out of the pages of a catalogue; his idea of "comfortable" a red-checked button-down shirt, chinos and elegant chestnut-brown dress shoes.

Adrenaline still coursing through her veins, she took a big, bold step his way. He didn't budge, though his chin lifted, and he slid his hands into the pockets of his chinos.

"Come on, Armand. Admit it. That was fun.

You, Mr Grouchy Pants, had fun. With me. Because we make a great team."

Nothing. Not a high five. Not even a nod.

"I think it has a lot to do with our motto," she said.

A single eyebrow kicked north. "We have a motto?"

"Yes, we do." She took another big step his way until she was close enough to nudge the toes of her polka-dot lace-ups against the toes of his fancy shoes. Then made a banner in the sky with her hand. "No man—or woman—left behind."

"I think you'll find that motto belongs to another. The American Army Rangers, I do believe."

"*Pfft.* Sharers are carers."

"You be sure and let them know that's how you feel."

Evie tipped a few millimetres closer. "For the last few years I've pretty much worked in a room all by myself. This kind of 'squad goal' moment is a rarity. And I plan to revel in it."

Armand looked down into her eyes. All dark and French and achingly gorgeous. Then his toe nudged against hers. Deliberately. And it was one of the sexiest moments of her life.

"Hey."

Evie glanced sideways to find Jamie and his cohorts rocking up to them, with a kid wearing an Escape Room Challenge T-shirt in tow. She leapt back a step. But it was too late. The look on Jamie's face said it all.

She held her breath as she awaited his reaction. When he gave her a smile and a wink the relief was palpable.

"You guys rocked," said the Escape Room kid, his voice breaking only a little. "That was totally a record, you know."

"A record, you say?" Evie bumped Armand with an elbow. "Doesn't that make us the best team that ever was?"

The kid said, "Um, yeah. I guess. Anyway, you win a certificate. A team laser-tag session."

"Seriously? That's awesome. Thanks!" She glanced up at Armand to find he was watching her, a small smile playing about his mouth. Not quite as big as the smile he'd smiled in the darkness of the Escape Room, but it made the butterflies kick up a notch all the same. "Hey, any chance we could use this now?"

The kid shrugged. "I guess. Next session starts in half an hour."

"Armand, Jamie, guys, what do you say?" Evie tugged her hair back into a ponytail. "We eat. We hydrate. And then we shoot at one another with lasers."

"We're in," said Jamie, bouncing about like a puppy. His crew concurred.

"Armand? Remember our motto."

She knew there was a chance he'd make an excuse. That his instinct was to edge away from the group. Then she saw the way the others looked up to him. Realised it would have been that way his whole life. The burden of leadership. She wondered then if he'd lost men during his Foreign Legion years. The chances were high. It would make making friends harder. Make letting people close harder still.

Before she could stop herself she reached out and took his hand, curling her fingers into his and drawing him back into the group. Showing him he wasn't alone in this.

He looked down at her, the bruise in his eyes gentling.

After a few long beats, he cricked his neck. "Let's do this."

"Woohoo!"

# CHAPTER NINE

BY THE TIME they left the arcade a light drizzle had begun to fall.

Once again Armand called a car and insisted Evie take it home. In the spirit of their motto, she insisted he do the same.

The ride was electric, buzzing with leftover adrenaline from their Escape Room win, their laser-tag demolition and whatever additives were in the chicken wings. Add the hum of tension that had been building between them all night— starting with small "accidental" touches and furtive glances and ending with their hands sitting millimetres from one another on the car seat— Evie felt as if her blood were filled with soda bubbles.

When the car pulled up outside Zoe's apartment, she turned to Armand. "Thanks for the ride. And for staying. It was a good night."

"Thanks for making me stay. And goodnight it is."

Evie shot him a look. He gave her one back.

"Fine. Goodnight. See you tomorrow."

He made the car wait until she'd run to the front of the building and opened the door.

Laughing, giddy, she waved him off, watching the car head around the corner to take him to wherever it was he spent his nights. She knew it was in South Yarra somewhere, as that was his train stop. But knowing some of his background now—from an idyllic childhood to growing up surrounded by priceless works of art, to his years living in the most basic, uncomfortable, dangerous places in the world—she had no clue as to the kind of place Armand would choose to call home.

She brushed raindrops off her puffer jacket and beanie and took the stairs two at a time to Zoe's third-floor apartment, unlocked the door and walked in on Zoe and Lance getting it on.

"Oh, no. Oh, jeez. Sorry, sorry, sorry!"

Eyes burning with the image of a naked backside and so many limbs writhing on the futon—*her* futon!—Evie somehow made it back out of the door and into the hall. She slammed the door shut and leant against it as if it might hold back the horror.

"Evie!" Zoe called, her voice muffled through the closed door. "I didn't know he was coming back. It was a surprise visit. I should have messaged you, or put a note on the door, but things kind of got out of hand fast."

"It's fine," said Evie flapping a hand in the direction of her friend's voice. "Look, I'll get out of your hair for the rest of the night."

"No! Don't be silly. Come back in."

"Not happening."

"Where will you stay?"

She hadn't made all that many friends since moving to Melbourne. Working on her own at her last job, she'd done little more than wave on her way in and out. After the Eric fallout, even those she'd been friends with on social media had slunk away.

But she'd never needed much. Been happy with little.

It hit her then how much things were about to change.

Keeping her voice as calm as humanly possible, Evie said, "I'll get a hotel room in the city for the night. Easy-peasy! Maybe something a little flash. A little gift to myself for getting the new job."

"Are you sure?" said Zoe, cricking open the door.

Evie looked over her shoulder to find Zoe wrapped in a blanket from the back of the futon. One she'd knitted. One she would never again pull over herself while watching TV. "Positive. It was always a matter of time."

Zoe sniffed. Her big blue eyes welling up. "I kind of imagined you living here for ever. Like a maiden aunt. Or a favourite pet."

Evie laughed, even as it turned into a sob. "I've loved every second of it."

"Me too."

"Lance better treat you like a princess."

"And I'll treat him like a prince."

Evie gave Zoe a quick kiss and hug before stepping back. "I'll talk to you tomorrow, okay? Bye, Lance!" she called through the door.

"Bye, Evie," he called back.

Hooking her backpack over her shoulder, Evie headed off back down the stairs, heart thundering in her chest, thoughts fluttering uselessly inside her skull. She checked her watch to find it close to ten.

With no car she did all she could do and walked to the train station.

The air was still filled with drizzle—the kind that seeped slowly into one's clothes until your entire body felt soggy. By the time she got to the station, rivulets of water dribbled down her back and her shoes were soaked through.

The platform was empty. Eerie. All concrete

greys, mossy greens and sharp, gleaming blacks, as if the warmth function in a photo app had been turned right down.

Pulling her icy hands deeper into the sleeves of her jacket, Evie nudged her toes against the yellow safety line and sniffed. But it wasn't the cold. A tear leaked from the corner of her eye and she dashed it away.

What the heck was she doing? Where did she think she was going?

She might have convinced Zoe, but the truth was she didn't have money to burn on a last-minute hotel. Not with the fact she was only on a contract and the price of her granddad's accommodation. And now Lance was back, what about tomorrow night and the next and the next?

She'd have to dip into her Just in Case account. Just in Case everything went wrong. She was her mother's daughter after all.

Which was why the fortune cookie had hit her hard.

From the moment she'd arrived in Melbourne, Evie had been waiting for the other shoe to drop.

She'd done her best to mitigate any possible disasters.

Working at a job she could have done in her sleep.

Staying on Zoe's futon.

Dating men she had no hope of losing her head over.

Her mother had been the opposite, leaving home at seventeen. Refusing to "get a real job" as she held tight to her dream of being an artist, sketching portraits at markets, busking with chalk art on the streets, sleeping wherever she landed each night.

Till she'd fallen in love, fallen pregnant and fallen on hard times. All that potential was for naught because she'd been in such a rush to live she'd tripped over her own feet.

Evie stared down the train tracks towards the city.

Choosing the comfort of familiarity over the risk of adventure hadn't made a lick of difference to Evie's story. Life had risen up and smacked her on the head anyway.

And yet… Maybe that was exactly what she'd needed.

She'd never have presumed to try for a job at Game Plan if she hadn't lost her last job so spectacularly. She'd probably have lived on Zoe's awfully uncomfortable futon for ever if circumstance wasn't forcing her to get off her butt.

The fortune cookie hadn't been a curse. It had been a revelation.

What it came down to now was whether or not she could follow that through. Continue taking safe, small steps through life, or surrender to adventure? Leap and discover how high she could go?

The lights at the end of the track began to flash. The screech of metal on metal cut through the chill night air and the train rumbled up to the platform. When the train doors opened she leapt inside. Found a random seat, tossed her backpack next to her and pulled out her phone.

She rolled it around in her hand once, twice, then with a hard, sharp out-breath pulled up the number she needed.

Three rings later, a delicious French voice answered. "Evie? What's wrong? I saw you go inside—"

"I did. I'm fine. I'm sorry to call so late but—"

"What is it?"

"Lance is back. I walked in on him and Zoe… together." She shut her eyes, but the image was indelible. "Anyway, I've let them be for the night. I'm on the train heading back into the city. And…"

And what, exactly? Her gut had told her to call Armand, but to what end?

*Adventure!* her heart cried.

But she hadn't stopped to consider that there was a really good chance he wasn't riding the same wave of revelation she was. He was still Armand. A lone wolf, brooding over internal bruises earned miles outside the boundaries of her own realm of experience.

Seeing a sliver of time in which to still save face, she opened her mouth to ask him to forget she had ever called when his voice rumbled over the phone.

"Stay there," he said, 'I'll turn the car around."

"I'm already on the train."

"You walked there? It's raining."

"And I wondered why I was wet."

He mumbled something under his breath in French.

"Are you sure about this?" Evie asked.

"I have a spare room. You will stay with me."

He hadn't answered her question, but she let it be. "Thank you. It'll be one night, I promise."

"Get off at South Yarra Station."

"Yes, sir."

"Evie," he chided.

"Fine. Yes. I'll do that. And I know which is

your stop, Armand." And maybe it was the snug cocoon of the train with the rain drizzling down the windows, or the soothing rocking of the carriage, but Evie found herself adding, "I've been well aware since the day you started taking my train."

"Is that so?"

"I even remember what you were wearing."

His quiet was loaded. Electric. She half thought he'd change the subject and yet found herself unsurprised when he said, "I'm assuming it was a suit of some description."

"It was."

"Of course, I have no idea which, so I'd have no hope of confirming or denying."

"Grey," she said, remembering the way the sunlight dappled the thread. "Subtle checked shirt. Green tie with white polka dots and matching—"

"Pocket square," Armand cut in.

The train slowed. Evie pressed her feet into the floor to counter the rocking. "I'd never seen a real live contemporary human person with a pocket square before. I thought you so dashing."

"Dashing?" he growled.

"With a healthy dose of mad, bad and dangerous to know."

Soft, rough laughter eased through the phone, sending waves of warmth through her all the way to her numbed toes.

Then Armand's voice sounded far away as he said something to the driver, no doubt asking him to take a different turn.

Evie sat up as a handful of people hopped onto the train. She shot them a polite smile as they passed, settling into the seat a few up from hers.

"Armand?"

"Hmmm."

"Thanks for this. I really appreciate it. You won't even know I'm there."

Again with the pause. As if he very much believed otherwise.

"I'll see you soon," he said, the phone clicking as he rang off.

Evie breathed out hard.

It had been a conversation. About getting a lift. From a workmate. Then begging a room for the night. But in that moment she understood how Zoe's phone had kept her and Lance happily together for years.

Evie slowly dropped her phone into her lap, turning it over and over between her hands, before looking out of the window. With the night having well and truly closed in, all she saw was her reflection looking back at her. Dark eyes, dark hair, nuclear-green beanie with a radiation patch sewn into the front.

For a moment she caught a rare glimpse of her mother in her own face.

She remembered her more from photographs nowadays. But she knew she had her mother's jaw, the splotch of gold in one iris, the shape of her smile.

The night she'd opened the fortune cookie she was at a dinner celebrating her twenty-sixth birthday. The same age her mother had been when she'd died.

The burden of which was not lost on her. Quite the contrary.

Maybe that was the message the universe had been trying to send her. It was time to go hard or go home.

Armand stood in the entrance to his apartment, tossing his keys from one hand to the other as he watched Evie take a turn about the room.

Not one to stand back, she ran fingers over the back of the soft leather couch, opened cupboards as she meandered through the warm, modern kitchen, took a spin beneath the repurposed chandelier. Her big, blue, puffy jacket squeaked as the cheap fabric swished together, the pom-pom on top of her beanie bobbing soggily.

"Jonathon put you up here?" she asked.

"Not exactly."

He'd refused payment from Jonathon, even in the form of rent, choosing instead to invest in a property in his company's name. First thing he'd done in that capacity in over a year, and it had felt good.

Working as a favour was not something he made a habit of, knowing what his skills were worth. But he'd needed the sense of autonomy. The surety he could walk away at any time. In case it turned out he was more broken than he'd realised. In case he was beyond repair.

"It's lovely, Armand," she said. "Not what I expected at all."

"And what was that?"

"Either four bare walls, an army cot, a box full of rations. Or a mini-Versailles." She shot him a smile, the kind that always left him feeling winded.

Which was when he noticed how much she was shivering.

He swore beneath his breath then strode over

to where she was. Without thinking he ran his hands down her arms, friction creating warmth.

"You're wet through."

"Rain will do that to a girl."

"How far did you walk?"

"A kilometre or so."

He looked around. "Where is your luggage? Did you leave it in the car?"

"I left in a bit of a hurry," she said, teeth chattering. "No clothes. Just my backpack and me."

He turned her around and moved her towards the spare room which came with its own *en suite* bathroom.

"Your bed," he said, facing her that way as they passed it, then he quickly turned her and walked her into the bathroom.

"Whoa. That's bigger than Zoe's whole apartment."

He peeled the backpack strap from her shoulder, dumped the bag on the stool at the end of the bed and then pressed her into the bathroom. When he realised the next step was stripping her down he let go. Took a step back.

She turned to face him, all damp lashes and hair dripping in straggled ribbons down the front of her jacket. Her make-up had smudged, making her big brown eyes look huge. Her lips were swollen, tipped slightly open as her teeth clattered together.

She took a deep breath in, the breath out rough and jagged. And there was a new light in her eyes—a mania, a hunger. As if a switch had been tripped.

Which was when Armand realised that while he had been blithely convinced he had a handle on his affections towards her, it had been she who'd been in charge of the pace. Giving him the room to want, to imagine, to lean in. To be less mindful of his own boundaries.

And now she'd taken her foot off the brake.

He could have put her up in a hotel. Or she could have slept at the office. Jonathon clearly did not have a problem with the practice, as Armand had walked into Montrose to find IT guys sleeping on beanbags, on couches, at their desks nearly every morning he'd been there.

Knowing she was in trouble, he'd wanted her safe. Needed her close. Because he'd doltishly let himself care.

Nonplussed, he dug deep, regathered his self-control and took another step back. Mumbled, "I'll put some clothes on the bed," and walked away, shutting the *en suite* bathroom door decisively behind him.

\* \* \*

Evie stared at the space where Armand had been before he'd scampered away.

Did he think she was going to jump him? He'd been in the French Foreign Legion, for Pete's sake. He could probably take her down with one finger.

She shivered at the thought, and not out of fear.

A quick reconnaissance uncovered a heat lamp in the bathroom. The difference was immediate, and welcome. She stripped off her jacket, her damp T-shirt. Nudged off her filthy, wet shoes and socks and climbed into the huge shower.

A long, hot shower brought her back to life, after which she wrapped herself in a fluffy bathrobe and tucked a towel around her damp hair.

She opened the bathroom door slowly, found herself alone.

Biting back a grin, she jumped into the bed—was there a size bigger than king? All those pillows! Oh, the sheets. The softest blanket she'd ever felt. After years spent sleeping on a futon, she nearly wept.

When she was done luxuriating she grabbed her backpack, fished out her phone and sent Zoe a quick message to let her know she had a roof over her head. After checking the time she made a quick call.

Her granddad—always an early bird on the farm, now very much a night owl at the retirement village—answered the phone with, "Well, if it isn't my little Evie Marie Saint. Christmas Evie. Happy Evie After."

"Hey, Granddady-O. I can hear noise. Where are you?"

"Playing Mah-Jong. Evie says hello!"

A chorus of voices met her. Mostly female.

"All right with you, love?"

"Sorry I didn't call this week. It's been a bit busier than usual here."

"Busy is good. Means you're settling in. Making a real life for yourself. That's all I need to know."

Evie rested her palm over her eyes, closing them against the knowledge she hadn't been doing that at all.

She asked after his friends in the village. Took the usual beanie requests. And finished off by saying, "If you need me, call my mobile."

"Problems with the landline?"

"Something like that."

She could have just told him she was staying with a friend, but the word felt all wrong. Though what else could you call someone who let you stay in their spare room without pause or hesitation? Maybe there was no word. Maybe it was bigger than words.

The conversation hit a pause. After which her granddad's voice softened. "Was there something else, love?"

"Um… I was thinking about Mum tonight. More than usual, I mean."

"Were you, love?"

Evie realised the background noise was quieting, meaning he'd found a private place to sit.

"I miss her," Evie said.

"As do I. There is no shame in that. Or in not thinking about her every day. Or in feeling like you've forgotten more than you can remember. It's normal. It's how it's meant to be."

"What about spending an inordinate amount of time making sure I don't make the same mistakes she made? Is that normal too?"

"And what mistakes would those be?"

"Falling for the wrong guy. Falling pregnant. Slinking home."

"Oh, love. She'd never have called any of those things mistakes. Your mother never did anything she didn't want to do. Including being with your father. Including having you. And yes, even including slinking back to the drudgery of the farm."

"I didn't mean—"

"I know, love. I was joshing with you. The years I had the both of you home with me were some of the best of my life. And hers. If you'd had the chance to ask her yourself she'd tell you the same."

Evie wiped a finger under her eye.

"Why do you think I keep telling you to sell the farm?" Granddad added. "I knew how much you wanted to go, while fretting I'd feel like you'd left me behind. Know that I'm happy here. Happier still knowing you're happy there."

Evie squeezed her eyes shut tight. He'd known, clever man. She hadn't been making a life for herself. She'd been preparing to flee at a moment's notice.

Well, no more.

"Thanks, Granddaddy-O."

"Anytime, All About Evie."

"Go back to your game. Show those ladies what it's all about."

"Will do."

Evie said her goodbyes and rang off. Feeling light and heavy. Young and old. As if she was at a tipping point in her life. Maybe it was the amazing bedding playing tricks with her mind.

A soft knock came at the door.

She wriggled off the end of the bed, fixed her gown, took the towel from her hair and ran quick fingers through the damp mess. Then said, "Come in."

Armand pressed the door open but did not enter—keeping himself very much on the right side of the threshold. He had a neat pile of what looked like flannel pyjamas in his arms.

"No suit?"

The corner of his mouth kicked up. And every part of her that hadn't yet defrosted did as a wave of heat rolled down her body.

"Heard you talking. Zoe?"

"My granddad. I make sure to call him a few times a week. Not that he needs me to. The man's more social than a teenager."

"I'm sure he needs you plenty," said Armand in that deep, delicious voice of his.

"Yeah. That's what I've always told myself. But he's the strongest man in the world."

"Did you tell him you are here?" Armand asked as he stepped into the room.

Evie's heart stuttered. "Ah, no. I haven't even told him I've changed jobs, either. He's strong but he's not young. If he knew I was in flux, he'd worry."

"You don't think he believes in you enough to know you would work it out?"

Evie's mouth twisted. "I'm just beginning to see that. Turns out I'm the one who didn't believe in myself."

His frown was so very French. "And what is there not to believe? You are resilient, no? Determined. When Jonathon hesitated, you did not take no for an answer. And you are stubborn, oh, yes. Sure of your talents. Loyal too. Look how much you care for Zoe and her man, walking through driving rain to give them space. You are inclusive and tolerant, lovely and kind."

Evie wondered if Armand realised his words had trailed off course there at the end. She had to swallow, her throat was so tight with emotion.

She walked over to him and slid the neat pile of pyjamas from his hands. Then she tossed them onto the bench at the end of the bed before turning back to him. "You think I'm lovely?"

Armand's eyes darkened and he breathed out hard through his nose. Evie's pulse responded with a scattered whumpety-whump.

"That's what you chose to take from all I said?"

She lifted one shoulder in a shrug. "Maybe a

little more. And maybe it's not actually that I don't believe in myself. I do. But I've come to realise I've been *acting* as if I don't. I've been careful—with work, places, people. I've not backed myself and taken any risks."

Armand watched her closely. Close enough now she could separate the shards of blue from grey in his volatile eyes. She could tell he was mulling over her words but she wasn't a mind-reader. She was rather glad of it as she said, "Except, that is, when I'm with you."

Armand's throat worked.

"I'm pushier, sharper, more bolshie. I don't know why."

She thought he might just stand there, all gorgeous and dark and impenetrable.

Then his voice came to her, soft and rough, as he said, "Don't you?"

"Because you push my buttons?"

"Because you sense that you can push mine as hard as you like and I won't break."

She breathed out hard. "Anyone can break."

His nostrils flared. His voice was barely a rumble as he said, "I've been close, so many times. Becoming so brittle I believed one more hit and I might shatter. Knowing too many people needed me to allow that to happen, I hid myself away, went deep into self-protect mode. Until I stepped onto a train one morning, heading into a foreign city, and saw a girl who looked as though she was made of light."

Evie's breaths were hard to come by. "Please don't say something like that just to make me feel better—"

"Your beanie was pink," he said, stepping forward to run a finger under a swathe of damp hair. His dark gaze followed the movement as he tucked her hair behind her ear. "The kind of pink that only exists in candyfloss."

Evie stopped breathing as her lungs shut down. She had a beanie in that colour. And had worn it a few weeks ago.

"There was something on top," said Armand, plucking at an imaginary tuft above Evie's head.

"A ball of feathers," Evie finished, her entire body pulsing with every heartbeat.

"You laughed as the train turned a corner, and the shaft of sunlight that washed over you seemed to bask in your warmth. Your laughter echoed inside me that entire first day at work. I hung on to it, like a vine at the edge of quicksand. You were a signpost showing me the way out. I could either continue to exist in a world of grey or decide to see the world through a new lens."

"Armand…" Evie began, but she had no idea what to say. Except the truth. "I've never met anyone like you before. You are far more than I'm used to."

"As are you to me," he said. "And yet here we are."

Then slowly, achingly slowly, he dropped his lips to hers. Pausing a millimetre from the promised land. His dark gaze capturing hers. "Is this what you want, *ma chérie*?"

She knew what he was asking. She'd made it clear how determined she was not to start anything with someone from work. But that train had left the station.

*Yes, yes, yes,* a voice whispered in the back of her mind, and this time it was her own.

She tipped up onto her toes and closed the gap, her mouth brushing against his. Once, twice. Tentative as a butterfly unfurling its wings for the first time.

And then Armand took over. Tilting her face to better fit his mouth to hers. Sipping on her, gently, slowly, tenderly—until her whole body whimpered with a need for more.

The hand on her cheek slid down her neck, over her collarbone, tracing the edge of the bulky gown.

Evie's head tipped back as Armand's mouth followed, so gentle, so thorough, she could barely keep her head. Air hard to come by, senses reeling, all she could do was feel. To risk. To live.

Shifting closer, his knee nudged hers and she stepped back, the backs of her knees knocking into the edge of her bed.

Without overthinking, following all possible paths in her mind in order to find the safest route, she let herself fall. And fall. And fall.

# CHAPTER TEN

EVIE WOKE THE next morning with an all-body stretch. When her hands and feet kept going without meeting lumps or edges of a futon her eyes snapped open.

Sunlight streamed through plantation shutters onto a moulded ceiling a mile above the bed. She looked over to find a second pillow with the indentation of a head. But no head. No Armand. The scent of freshly brewed coffee told her he was around somewhere.

She grabbed the pillow and hugged it to her chest, squeezing her eyes shut tight as memories of the night before bombarded her like a movie-highlights reel: the feel of his hot skin under her hands. The warmth of his mouth on her. The way he'd curled himself around her, protecting her as she slept.

Feeling herself dropping off in drowsy bliss, Evie forced herself to roll out of bed and turned on the shower. Only once she went to get dressed did she realise the only clothes she had were the ones she'd worn the night before. If she wasn't careful it was going to be a serious walk of shame.

She grabbed her phone to text Zoe, in the hopes

they'd make the same train, but Zoe had already messaged:

Sorry about last night. But thank you. Taking a sickie today. Can't get out of bed.

So much for that idea. In the end she turned her dinosaur shirt inside out and back to front and hoped for the best.

Downstairs, Armand was already dressed—in the bottom half of a suit and a white T-shirt, his shirt, tie and jacket hanging over the back of a kitchen stool. He leant against the kitchen bench, eating a croissant and reading an actual old-fashioned newspaper.

Her heart clutched, sputtered and flipped over on itself. She tried to swallow but her throat was too tight.

What had she done to deserve such a man?

Not that he was *hers*. *Pfft*. Not at all! They'd spent a night together. The most wonderful, tender, amazing night of her life.

But no matter what happened from here, it paid to remind herself he'd be heading back to France when the job was done. Meaning this…whatever it was, had a ticking clock.

It would end—just as her last job had ended, her last apartment had ended. Being strong enough to be with Armand and then to watch him walk away—that was the last step in her transformation. Into knowing she was living her own life, for real.

She must have made a sound—probably something between a sigh and a sob—as Armand looked up. His eyes gleamed before his mouth curved into a smile. "Good morning, Evie."

She couldn't help herself; she grinned like an idiot. "Hi. Any more where that came from?"

He reached over and grabbed a plate piled high with croissants. And carried them over to her. She plucked one off the top—no, two—and took a bite. He put the plate back down, then leaned over and kissed the top of her head.

"Coffee?" Armand asked as he pushed away from the bench.

Evie pressed his back, her fingers lingering a moment as she remembered the glory of all that warm skin and hard, curving muscles beneath the shirt. "Let me."

She saw the fight in him, the difficulty he had letting someone else be in charge. Before something relaxed in him and he said, *"D'accord."*

She worked out how to use the espresso machine quick smart, grabbed cream over milk and proceeded to make two coffees.

"*Merci*," he said when she handed his over, offering up the most glorious smile. Private, intense, scorching.

"Any time," she said.

Then Armand looked over her shoulder and swore, in French, and motioned to the clock.

She took a few quick gulps of yoghurt, downed her espresso in one steaming, bitter shot. Then ran around like a lunatic, tracking down her jacket, her beanie, her shoes. "Armand, have you seen my...? Oh." There they were, resting by the fireplace, all dry and toasty warm. She sank down onto the floor to pull her shoes over her chilly feet and she sighed in bliss. "Oh, I love you for this!"

The silence that met her was palpable. She slowly glanced over to find Armand watching her as he buttoned his shirt.

"I didn't mean—"

"I know."

"It just came out." She pulled herself to her feet. "I barely know you. You could have a wife and kids back in Paris for all I know." *Please don't let there be a wife and kids.* "These are things a person really should find out before falling into bed with some random guy."

Armand simply waited for her to finish, his gaze forbearing.

"Well, not *random*," she ameliorated. Not even close. If she could have picked any man in all the world to have spent the night before with she'd have picked him. Not that she was about to tell him. She might have been in the habit of making mediocre choices but she wasn't completely self-destructive.

"I'm single," he said. "Divorced, to be precise. No children."

"Really?" she said, one eyebrow raised. Maybe they should have labelled him Mr Mysterious. "Divorced, huh? What happened?"

He looked at her as if he had no intention of going there, before, for some reason, he relented. "I disappointed her. It's one of my more consistent skills. Disappointing those who do love me."

Evie swallowed. "Not possible."

"Believe it. Lucia was the aunt of the little girl on that first kidnapping rescue. She imagined my life was drama and heroism and fell for the romance of her vision. After five years of soldiering, I fell for the mirage of having someone to come home to. She never forgave me for refusing to play the hero. Just as my family never forgave me for refusing to play the good son in the first place and take over the Debussey auction houses."

Evie got one arm through her jacket before stopping. "That makes no sense to me. How could they all get you so wrong? You're not a player—in any sense of the word. *Hero* is an overused word, so I won't go there. But anyone who knew you and found themselves disappointed…? I'd like to meet them so they can tell me so to my face."

He watched her eyes as she spoke, his gaze hot and pointed, as if he was trying to see into her very soul. And something in his eyes made the next question one of the hardest she'd ever had to ask. "Where is she, Armand? Where's Lucia?"

"She was killed a little over a year ago."

Evie's hand swept up to her mouth but not in time to cover the groan. "Oh, jeez. Armand, I'm so sorry."

Armand fixed the face of his watch until it sat just so. "We'd parted years before. One day she packed her bags and left and it didn't even occur to me to stop her. Last year we reconnected at one of my family's charity events, both apologising for having not put an end to things far sooner. A week later she was mugged. Stabbed while trying to wrest back her handbag. She bled to death before the ambulance arrived."

Oh, Armand. No wonder he brooded. No wonder he'd looked so bruised when she'd kissed him. He would have taken it all on himself.

Evie took a step his way. "She sounds like a very strong woman. To have fought back. Quite the hero herself."

He ran both hands down his face and looked her way again. "She'd have liked that."

"Do you think you might have become more to one another again, if…if it hadn't happened?"

Armand shook his head. "We were the result of a rare weak moment."

Evie felt as if a fist squeezed around her heart. Was that what was happening here? Would he look back and think the same of her one day?

Needing to lighten the room, to let him off the hook, she said, "Is that how Jonathon got you over here? Another moment of weakness?"

His mouth twitched. "Something like that."

"Well, I'm glad. About Jonathon. Bringing you here. Not the rest. Though without the rest you wouldn't be here. A butterfly flaps its wings… and I'm going to stop talking now." A beat then, "Except to say that I'm truly sorry. For all that happened. And that your family doesn't see you for all that you are. And I'm single too, in case you wondered."

She pulled a face and told herself to *please* stop

talking. And she would, after she said one more thing. "Look, I want you to know that I didn't come here for…last night."

"And I didn't offer my room for…last night."

Her pause had been a case of sudden-onset modesty. His pause made her think of tangled sheets and slippery limbs and gasps of air as time held its breath.

"If you like we can shake hands and part ways, go back to annoying one another in our tiny office and pretend nothing happened."

"But something did happen," said Armand.

"Yes, it did."

"You were the one who said I'm not a player. It means I'm no good at pretending. Let's not attempt it."

Evie couldn't stop her grin. "Okay, then."

He tilted his chin. "Grab your things, *ma chérie*, it's time to go."

Evie quickly made sure she had everything she'd come with, looking around in case it was the last time she saw the place. Her heart squeezed at the thought. But she knew it wasn't the lovely apartment she would miss.

Armand pulled on his jacket with an elegant swish, then met her at the door. Where he took her by the hand and pulled her into his arms.

Her eyes opened in surprise in time to see his close as he kissed her, hard and strong, his tongue sliding over the seam of her mouth until she opened to him and allowed him to sweep her away.

No sign of the tender touch and slow burn of the night before. He had her so hot she didn't even realise she was trying to climb him like a tree until he loosened his grip.

When he pulled back her legs had gone limp and she grabbed him by the lapels of his jacket, giving her time to find her feet.

"Stay here tonight."

It was not a question.

"No. It'll be fine. I'll check in with Zoe to see if we can make it work for a bit, till I find a new place."

Armand just looked at her.

"What?" she said.

"Lance has been on tour for how long?"

"I'll find a cheap hotel on a train line in the suburbs."

"Not necessary."

"I can't stay here, Armand. The noticeboard at work has a couple of rooms-to-let notices. I think one might be Jamie's—"

Evie squealed as Armand wrapped an arm

around her waist and hauled her in close, his nose pressed up against hers. Forehead too.

"You are not staying with that *goujat*."

"*Goujat?* What's that?"

"Bounder. Hound. Woof-woof."

"Ah. I thought you two had made friends."

"My friend is a hound. It's decided; you stay here. *Oui*?"

"*Oui*," she said, and he grinned, his eyes squinting a little, giving him smile lines. And just like that she fell a little more. A lot more. So hard and fast her head swam.

She'd only just started this adventure kick and already felt as if she had to hang on for dear life.

"No fancy car and driver today?" she asked when Armand strode towards the station.

"I like the train."

"Honestly? It's not some form of penance? Or undercover research?"

"Honestly."

Just when she thought she had a handle on him... She liked the train, but if she had the choice she'd totally take the luxury of a driver.

After another minute he said, "The train makes the travel time feel faster. The quiet in the car can be too much."

"Don't like to be left alone with your own thoughts?"

He glanced at her, that now familiar expression of surprise. Then, "Yes. White noise is better."

Before she could stop herself, Evie slid a hand into the crook of Armand's elbow. He put a hand over the top and tucked her in tight. It had to be a French thing—this absolute self-confidence. No game-playing, no post-sex masculine posturing. It was a little overwhelming. And a whole lot lovely.

"I like seeing the same people each day," said Evie. "It's like following a soap opera."

"Soap opera?"

"A daytime drama. Where you become invested in their lives."

Armand smiled at her again and ushered her through the turnstile right as their train came along. By the time they got on, Armand's usual seat was free. Coincidentally so was hers. By unspoken agreement they remained standing somewhere in the middle.

"Careworn Mum," said Armand.

Evie glanced at the woman across the aisle with triplets climbing over her. "You name them? *I* name them!"

Though "careworn" was a far nicer way of

labelling the other woman's predicament than "frazzled".

"I wonder how she attempts this run every week," said Armand.

"The neighbours who rent my granddad's farm have young boys. Wildlings. Always better in open spaces than confined. What about those guys?" she asked, motioning to her usual pack of schoolboys on their phones.

Armand said, "I call them Fear for Our Future."

Evie laughed. "Even you were like that when you were fifteen."

"I was never like that."

She laughed, believing him.

But then she wondered—*had* he always been so self-contained? Or had the big, dark moments of his life shaped him so drastically they had hacked at his compassion, rubbed away any softness, leaving him unrelentingly unmoved?

Was that why she had ultimately been so drawn to him? Because it was clear any "moments of weakness" would be rare. A man like that could never break your heart, as a man like that would never hold it in the first place.

Armand caught her eye, his eyebrow rising in question. He saw right through her and always had. Meaning he probably knew exactly how she felt. Even before she did.

She cleared her throat before saying, "Do you think that means that they all name us too?"

"It's possible."

"What might we be? I'm probably Knitting Woman. Or Beanie Girl. Or… Hang on a second. You've called me something a couple of times now. What was it?"

"The Girl with the Perfect Aim."

Evie grimaced then laughed. "Right. Your foot."

"And my solar plexus."

"I was hoping you'd forgotten that."

"Never."

Another gap of quiet, though this one felt less empty. There was a strange kind of hum there now, filling the gaps. It was so lovely Evie felt like her smile was smiling.

Until Armand asked, "What did you call me?"

And like that Evie fell into her own trap. No way was she about to give up the fact she'd called him Hot Stuff in the Swanky Suit. Or—heaven forbid—her Train Boyfriend. She frantically searched for something believable.

What did he do, apart from sit there scowling, and looking gorgeous—?

"Reading Guy. We called you Reading Guy."

"Mmm..." he grunted. "That's fair."

*Phew.*

The winter sun shone over the artwork scrawled into the walls of the alleyway as they neared the Montrose offices. Armand wasn't sure he'd actually noticed the artwork before. Or that Jonathon's entrance was in an alley.

In fact, he tried to remember the last couple of dozen times he'd walked from the train station but it was a blur of grey. Shapes. Streets crossed. Corners turned. But today...

"Can you smell coffee?" he asked. "And buttered toast?"

Evie looked at him sideways. Then tipped her chin over his shoulder to the doorway of a café that seemed to have sprung suddenly from the wall to his right.

"Was that always there?"

"Not since the beginning of time, but yeah."

Armand only half heard, as his senses were all talking to him at once.

Birdsong in the roof gutters, car tyres whistling against the damp bitumen. The tell-tale rainbow shimmer of oil on the path ahead. The sun glinting off the threads in Evie's shiny jacket, the mis-shapen curve of her knitted hat.

Cool at his collar, Armand lifted his hand to find he'd forgotten to put on his tie.

"Look," said Evie, grabbing him by the elbow and pulling him up short. "Can we just have one more chat about this?"

"This?" The fact that everything was loud, bright, as if he'd stepped out of a sensory deprivation tank.

"This." She waved a frantic hand between them. "Back in your apartment the thought of being all *laissez-faire* sounded fine, but here..." She glanced up at the building. "When we go in there, can we just keep things normal?"

"Normal."

"I frustrate you. You ruffle me."

"That is true."

She glared at him a moment before bursting into laughter. He'd never known a person so quick to find joy. "I'm serious. I made such a big deal with the others about being one of the guys, if they found out you and I were..."

Armand reached up and tucked in the tag at the neckline of the T-shirt she'd put on back to front. "Worried I'll cramp your style?"

"Are you serious? My cred would level up."

She sank her face into both hands and gave her head a wild shake, dark hair floating over her shoulders. "But what about Jonathon? He put his faith in us to work together, not...you know. What if I lose his respect?"

A memory swam to the surface; Jonathon assuring him he Did Not Care if they did anything HR would not approve of. He tucked it back away.

"Evie, are you planning on embezzling from the company?"

Her head whipped up so fast her hair caught in her lashes.

"There she is," said Armand. "Will your work suffer because of last night?"

She held up finger and thumb and held them a millimetre apart.

Armand couldn't help but laugh. *Laugh*. Before coming to this part of the world he couldn't remember the last time he'd smiled.

"Your fifty percent is everyone else's one hundred, so that's a moot point. It is none of anyone's business. Including Jonathon. Yet you are determined we seal our lips?"

She nodded vigorously. Then her gaze dropped to his lips, her wide-open face giving him everything he needed to know.

"Then sealed they are," he said. "You Australians, so uptight."

Her gaze slunk back to his, eyes narrowed. Then she quickly checked the alleyway, lifted up onto her toes, kissed him hard and fast, then ducked through the door and inside.

Armand counted to thirty, looked into the camera that had no doubt filmed their entire conversation, gave it a jaunty wave, then opened the door and went to work.

"Mate."

Armand pulled up as Jonathon came out of his office. "Morning."

"Evie just scooted past like she had a dragon at her heels. Everything all right?"

"As far as I know."

Jonathon looked at him a moment. "Great. So how was last night?"

The fingers of his right hand curled into his palm until he realised Jonathon was asking about the Escape Room. Now who was acting uptight? "A corporate espionage soldier story? Subtle."

"Imogen found it. Worth her weight in microchips, that one. I hear you aced it. Jamie couldn't hold it in this morning. I think someone has a little crush."

Armand's fingers were again starting to tingle. "You only just noticed. He's had his eye on her from day dot."

Jonathon's mouth twitched. "I was talking about you. The kid totally wants to be you when he grows up."

Armand breathed out hard and counted to three. "Okay, then. I have a job to do—"

"All in good time. Now, what were we talking about?"

"When you think you might grow up."

"Right."

As one they turned to look over the railing at the Bullpen below, then they were off and running, reminiscing about their uni days, when growing up was the last thing on their minds. Deliberately leaving out the Turkish trip, during which they had both grown up overnight.

Again Armand only listened with half an ear but by then his senses had well and truly recalibrated. And they were twanging like a plucked violin string.

Something Jonathon said niggled at him. Not Jamie. Not this time. *Time*. He'd said "*All in good time*". The man was so concerned about his huge new project he'd all but cried on the phone to convince Armand to come all the way over here to help him, and now he was saying it could be sorted out "all in good time".

Out of the corner of his eye Armand catalogued Jonathon's fidgeting fingers, the way he shifted as if his shoes were too tight. The fact his gaze couldn't quite stick.

Dammit. Jonathon was hiding something. Knowing Jonathon, it could be anything—a new woman in his life, a new invention he'd patented, but it wasn't.

It was something to do with this project.

"Everything all right with you?" Armand asked when Jonathon took a breath.

"Sure, mate," he said. Silence hung between them, taut and loaded. Until Jonathon sparked up with his trademark grin. "Why do you ask?"

Armand considered pushing the matter. But he wasn't prepared to go into battle without a further reconnaissance. He pushed away from the railing. "I'd better get to it."

Jonathon glanced down the hall to where Evie was no doubt already hard at work and said, "Go get 'em, cowboy."

Evie stood beside Armand on the train platform, waiting for the evening ride back to his place.

He was busy scowling and texting on his ancient cell phone—it was painful to watch—so she left him be.

It had been the longest day of her life. Stuck in their small room, trying to concentrate on her work. She'd had to stop and go back more than once, which was not like her. In the end she'd begged if she could pack up her laptop and go to the cafeteria.

Fully expecting a blanket "not on your life" and a lecture on the importance of security, she'd found herself disappointed when Armand had suggested she ask Jonathon.

When Jonathon had told her to do whatever her heart desired, Armand's response was instant. Storm clouds rolled in and he'd grunted at her like in the days of old. Lucky she enjoyed that side of him. The caveman in the designer suit.

Deciding it was between them, she'd given Armand a quick kiss on the cheek before shooting off to the Yum Lounge. Surrounded by food and coffee, and a fort of chairs to keep the scavengers away, she'd powered through acres of code.

Either the problem was deeply hidden in striations within the code, or Jonathon, in fact, had himself a fantastic new product. She'd felt productive either way, until she'd headed back to the office to find Armand still fuming.

"Still don't want to tell me what has put a bee in your bonnet?" she asked.

He rolled a shoulder, checked his phone again and moved a little further up the train platform.

She rolled her eyes and followed, not about to let him go back into his mental man cave. For she couldn't quite work out how she'd managed to lure him out of there in the first place and wasn't sure enough of her own allure to know she could do it again.

"Armand, what's going on?"

"Nothing. Nothing important."

"I don't believe you."

"And yet I have nothing more to add."

She threw her hands in the air. "Is this the way it's going to be? Because I'm not going back to your place to hide in my room. I can do that at Zoe's."

His attention finally shot back to her. He reached out and took her by the elbow. Began to draw her in—

Then his phone rang. He looked at her—she could have sworn it was a look of fraught despair.

He let go and answered the phone. "Jonathon,

I've been trying to get you all damn day." Then he turned and moved further up the way.

Giving in, for now, Evie watched as two of the triplets she recognised as belonging to Frazzled Mum chased one another across the platform. She glanced back to find the mum coming along behind them, one boy asleep in the pram, the other seats filled with discount shopping bags.

Evie looked to see where Armand had gone when she saw he had stilled. His mouth moved as he spoke on the phone, his eyes on the boys as if he were a tiger preparing to pounce.

One toddler had hit the yellow line—the one behind which grown-ups knew to wait. The other, on the other hand…

Evie stepped forward, a country girl's instinct to help warring with a city girl's learned response to stay the heck out of other people's business.

Then the ground beneath her feet began to buzz, and rumble, and the clatter of metal wheels on train tracks split the air.

Everything from that moment happened in a blur.

Toddler number one stopped at the yellow line. While toddler number two saw his chance to win the race and kept on running, waddling to the edge of the platform before tipping right over the edge.

Someone screamed. It might even have been Evie.

The taste of bile rose up in her throat as fear and horror slammed her from all sides, her vision contracting to a tunnel as she ran to grab the other boy.

Before she was anywhere near him, Armand was at the edge of the platform, his coat flying out behind him like a cape.

Everything from that point slowed—as if it had been choreographed for a movie. He scooped up one toddler under his arm, handing the boy off to a random stranger. Then, with a glance up the tunnel, towards the now heavy rumbling and screeching of the oncoming train, he leapt onto the tracks.

Evie's heart slammed up into her throat. Her legs collapsed out from under her till she stumbled to her knees. But she didn't stop, crawling towards the edge, her usually sharp mind in a tailspin.

She would have followed him too—right over the edge—when out of the corner of her eye she saw the mother, mouth open in a silent scream, a bag of apples spilling from the pram and over the edge of the platform.

Evie was on her feet, with suddenly superhuman strength stopping the crying woman from hurling herself and her other boy onto the track too.

Then, with the screech of brakes and a siren tripped no doubt by Armand's leap, the commuter train braked hard as it barrelled into the station.

Evie slammed her eyes closed as she was hit with a blast of air from the train as it passed—relentless, unstoppable—smacking against her over-sensitised skin till she felt as if it was going to peel right off.

A million years later, the train finally stopped.

When Evie opened her eyes, it was to find the doors remaining closed. The people inside looking bewildered, talking and pointing towards the source of the siren splitting the otherwise deathly silence of the station.

Then, through the translucent train windows, she saw, on the far platform on the other side of the tracks, dark hair, a suit jacket, no tie. Armand. Hands on his knees, breathing heavily.

"They're okay," she said on a sob, grabbing the mother hard. "Both of them. They're okay."

"Are you sure?"

"Look," she said, pointing through the gaps to the other side of the train, where an official in a blue uniform had a crying two-year-old in her arms.

The mother broke down, her cries racking her in deep, thankful sobs.

The stranger to whom Armand had handed the first toddler came up to Evie and the mother. The mother grabbed her child, too shocked to say thank you.

The stranger gave Evie a look. A mix of shock and relief.

To which Evie mumbled, "You have no idea."

It was ages, *for ever*, before the doors opened and the commuters poured onto the platform, the siren still wailing.

Evie shifted to see through the window to find a mob of security guards with unhappy faces and dark uniforms talking into walkie-talkies and sweeping commuters back up the stairs, leaving the far platform clear.

In the centre was Armand. Organising, retelling, looking for all intents and purposes like a general. Till each guard shook his hand, or slapped him on the shoulder, then slowly moved away.

Armand stood looking out into the dark, dirty

well of the gap where the train now stood. He brought a hand to his mouth, held it there a moment, before wiping his face hard and putting both hands on his hips.

Then he lifted his gaze.

Through the dusty double windows, he found her.

The storm in his eyes...it had cleared. His shoulders were back. His breaths long and deep. As if he'd woken from a slumber.

"Let's get her to her baby," the stranger beside her said.

Evie nodded, taking the pram while the other stranger comforted the mother and they herded her towards the lift that would get them to the other platform.

Evie kept glancing over her shoulder, trying to catch Armand's eye once more.

She'd always known her brain was special. Quick and curious and clever. But in that moment, when the world had been about to tip into the worst kind of tragedy, compared to Armand her thoughts had been sluggish, like wading through thick mud.

He clearly didn't like to think of himself as heroic—merely fulfilling his duty—as a son, a

Frenchman, a friend. Didn't mean Evie couldn't quietly think it for him.

Evie managed to find a tight smile as she explained to the guard that both she and the woman with the pram needed to get down to the platform, investigation scene or not, and that nobody was going to stop them.

Her heart was thundering by the time the lift doors opened. When she saw Armand—big, dark and cool as a cucumber—the urge to run into his arms was only stoppered by the number of police with guns in their holsters milling about.

In the end it didn't matter, as Armand made a direct beeline for her. And said, "What the hell were you thinking?"

"Excuse me?"

Armand took her by the elbow and dragged her into a quiet spot around the corner by the stairs. "I saw what you were about to do. You were about to climb down there yourself."

"And?"

"You would have been killed."

"You made it."

"I am trained for that kind of thing!"

"Really? Is there a Rescuing Toddlers Who've Fallen onto Train Tracks Only Moments Before a Train Zooms into the Station battalion in the French Foreign Legion? That's lucky."

His cheek twitched but there was no humour in it. "This isn't funny."

"I never said it was, Armand. I'm the one who should be doing the yelling here, but I'm not because you were amazing. So amazing I could jump your bones, right here and now."

He looked at her with solemn dark eyes and she remembered belatedly what he'd told her about his ex. About how she'd been stuck on him "playing the hero". Dammit. That was not what she'd meant at all.

She was just deeply glad he was okay.

"We can go," he said, stepping back.

"Great. I just want to check on Frazzled Mum."

Which she did. The woman's husband was on his way. All three of her children had crayons and colouring books. And she was cradling a hot cup of tea.

She found Armand scowling at the bottom of the stairs, and without having to say a word they headed up to street level, where a car awaited them.

Not another word was said on the car ride back to Armand's apartment. There were no words.

Nothing he could say he would not wish to take back. The tension was loud enough, shimmering in the air around them like a mirage.

Once they were through the door the tension spilled over, and before he knew it Armand had Evie with her back to the wall and her leg around his waist as they kissed as if it was their last time.

He pulled back, dragging in breaths, placing a hand on the wall behind her head to steady himself, his jacket and hers in puddles at their feet. His shirt missing a button. Her hair like a wild, dark cloud about her face. His eyes lifted to hers and he'd never seen such emotion in his life.

Confusion and lust, worry and fear.

She sank a hand into his hair, holding him in place.

He waited for a continuation of the argument from the train station. In his experience that was how these things went.

But her voice was soft, emotional, rough as she said, "Take me to bed."

And just like that Armand's heart cracked in two. "You scared the hell out of me, Evie."

"I know."

"I scared the hell out of me too."

"What do you mean?"

"I haven't worked in the field in a long time. I

wasn't sure I could ever again. But since you... because of you... I feel like that part of me is back. That I can contribute. That I can help. I couldn't have done that without you."

"I did nothing," she said, her voice cracking. "I just stood there and watched. That little boy is alive because of you."

"And I," said Armand, "feel alive again because of you."

For this woman had switched him back on. Calling to his humanity, to the innocence he had spent years trying to bury. Leaving him looking not to yesterday, to regret, to how he could have done better, but to tomorrow and whatever it might bring.

"Armand," she croaked as a single tear rushed down her cheek.

He kissed it away.

Then lifted her off her feet and carried her to his bed. Where he felt every sensation, every touch, every smile and every tear in three dimensions and technicolour and made damn sure Evie felt the same.

# CHAPTER ELEVEN

AFTER SPENDING THE weekend in bed, Evie somehow made it to Monday.

She made herself a little nest on the couch at work—piling cushions around her back until she was comfortable. She made sure the plate of neatly lined-up chocolate buttons was within reach, clamped her headphones to her ears, found the playlist she'd made to connect her to the job and got to work.

Or at least she tried.

It was hard with Armand sitting behind his heavy wooden desk, banker's lamp streaming golden light over his sleek profile. Knowing the missing tie was all down to her.

"Need something?" he asked.

She quickly looked back at her laptop. "Hmm?" came her response, as if she hadn't been wholly attuned to his every blink, every breath, every scrape of fingernails over the stubble on his jaw.

Even after the transcendental weekend, during which Evie could safely say she'd never felt more real, more understood, more cherished by another human being in all her life, Armand was in a mood.

Not that she minded. It was that darkly delicious, stormy-eyed, messy-haired gravity that had drawn her to him in the first place. The urge to go over there, to climb on his lap and tame the tangles was a strong one.

"Everything okay over there?" she asked.

He didn't say a word.

"Armand?"

When he remained silent, still a niggle of concern edged its way past the bliss as she realised he was deep inside his cave. The person she had been a few weeks ago would have left him there and backed away quietly.

But she'd been willing to accept very little for so long—with regards to work, living arrangements, friendships. And he was the one who'd made her realise it didn't have to be that way.

She could risk big. She could close her eyes and leap. And falling wasn't always bad. Falling could be the ride of your life.

She put her laptop on the coffee table and ambled over to his desk, put both hands flat on the top and said, "Armand, if you don't tell me right now why you are so gloomy I'm going to make you."

He looked up and a glimmer flashed into his

eyes before being swallowed by the storm. "And how are you going to do that?"

"Scream? Stomp my feet? Go to Jonathon?"

The absolute quiet of his response sent a chill up her spine. This was no brooding; it was completely devoid of the passion that made him care so much.

Her gaze dropped to the papers gripped in Armand's hand. "What have you found?"

"Nothing."

She lifted a foot, ready to stomp, hoping to get a laugh out of him, or an answer. Anything but this stillness.

Then from one second to the next she realised what he meant. And the breadcrumbs in her mind lined up in a perfect row.

"There's nothing wrong with the program, is there?"

Armand slowly shook his head.

Evie smacked the table and bounced back. "Ha! I knew it. I mean, it was odd that I hadn't found even a single breadcrumb by now. Just a line of code here and there that needed streamlining. First I thought it was because Jonathon knew his stuff—that he'd bought some seriously sophisticated programming. But I had begun to think I was missing things because I was distracted. You are very distracting, you know. Now I can stop feeling guilty on that score. What do we do now?"

"We don't have to do anything."

"We have to tell Jonathon. He'll be stoked."

It took a few moments for Evie to realise that Armand had not said a word. He just gripped that piece of paper so hard his knuckles had turned white.

And it hit her. "He knows. He always knew." She threw her hands in the air and paced. "Why? Why would he do that to me? To us? To you? Was that the test? To see how long it would take us to figure it out?"

She stopped pacing and stared into the middle distance. "That might actually make sense."

Head spinning, Evie landed back on the couch with a bounce.

"Wow. Does this mean…?" Her waterfall of words came to a stop as she realised exactly what it meant. "It's over. The contract. The project. The team. No man—or woman—left behind."

She tilted her head to find Armand watching her. He looked—not sad, not angry. He looked empty.

Her skin came over cold, clammy. "You knew, didn't you?"

"I had begun to suspect."

"When?"

"A few days ago."

"A few... *What?*"

"The fact that I had found nothing—or more precisely that you had found nothing... It was too clean. Almost as if it had been homogenised. Like one of your games. Virtually real, only completely not."

"And why didn't you tell me then? In the shower this morning? On the train?"

Could it be because he too was feeling the squeeze around his chest, not knowing what this meant for them?

No. Not Armand. His response? "Because it's my fault."

Evie flinched. "What? No. Jeez, Armand. Not this time."

She pulled herself to standing and moved around behind Armand's desk, sitting on the edge. "Stuff happens. People fall pregnant, fall in love with the wrong people, die of aneurisms before they are even thirty. No matter how clever you are, how prepared, how big and strong, you can't protect everyone from everything. If it's anyone's fault, it's Jonathon's."

She reached over and pressed the red button on Armand's phone and yelled, "Jonathon!"

"What can I help you with, Ms Croft?" crooned his disembodied voice.

"Why don't you come on over and I'll tell you all about it?"

"I'll see you in a jiffy."

Evie shrugged at Armand. "See, we can sort this thing out in a jiffy?"

"Evie," Armand said, lifting out of his chair. No longer empty, his eyes were stormier than she'd ever seen them.

Her belly quivered at the sight. But she didn't have the chance to decipher if it was fear or lust making it happen as Jonathon burst through the door holding a coffee mug in his hand.

He took one look at them, Evie perched on Armand's desk, and Armand standing by her side, and smiled like the cat who'd found the cream. "What can I do for you?"

Evie looked to Armand but feared what he might do, so she spun around and said, "We were wondering why you've had us trying to find a problem in a program that has no problem."

"Whatever do you mean?"

"Jonathon." Armand had found his voice. "It's time to put an end to this."

After a few tense moments Jonathon looked to Evie and began a slow clap. "Well done you."

For half a second Evie thought about taking the applause when she saw her future—working for Game Plan, mentored by the man she'd called her hero. But that was before she'd known what that word really meant.

"It was Armand," she said. "He figured it out days ago."

"I don't doubt it. Cleverest man I know. Days ago, you say? Then I wonder why he didn't confront me sooner, don't you?"

Armand moved around Evie with the grace of a man half his size. "You know why."

"Tell me," Jonathon said. "Better yet, tell her."

Evie looked between them, realising there was an undercurrent slipping and sliding beneath their words. "Tell me what?"

Armand took a deep breath in and turned to face her, blocking her completely from Jonathon's view. "I didn't say anything because it would mean that this was over."

Evie made herself swallow. "Armand, that's sweet. But I knew once we were done here you'd be going home." She'd counted on it, needing to put this experience behind her so she could start her life afresh. Not that it stopped the pressure around her heart.

"I don't mean for me, Evie. It's over for you."

Evie made to look past him to Jonathon, but Armand moved, blocking her. Snagging her gaze and not letting go.

Armand's grip tightened on her arm before easing up, his body rigid with barely checked tension. "Jonathon didn't give you this job because he thought you were ready for it. He gave you the job for me."

"For you? I don't understand."

"He knew I was in a bad way. That I'd been living in a fugue for a long time. He brought me out here in an effort to wake me up. It wasn't working, until the day you came into his office. Don't you remember? When he saw us together he hired you on the spot."

"You *knew* this was why? And you let it happen anyway?"

"I thought he was being facetious. I'd convinced myself that the spark he'd claimed to see was all in his head. I was wrong."

Head spinning, heart aching, foundation shaking beneath her, Evie pushed Armand aside and stalked up to Jonathon Montrose. Her boss. Her one-time hero. Right now a person she wanted to smack. Hard.

"Is that true? Did you hire me as some kind of lure?"

Jonathon took a sip of his coffee while he considered his response. "I saw an opportunity for an interesting collaboration. I think we can all agree, here and now, that it worked a treat."

Evie's stomach sank and in the same breath anger so bright it filled her vision with a burning white light filled her entire body.

Before she knew it she was off the ground, legs kicking, arms flailing, as Armand lifted her bodily out of the way. "Let me at him," she cried. "You said you wanted to kill him with your bare hands at times. Let me at him."

"No," Armand crooned, "killing him won't solve anything. I'd rather see him suffer."

Then he gave her a smile, his mouth kicking up at one side, his eyes glinting in that way that made her feel as if to him she was a natural wonder.

When she went limp he held her close and let her slide down his body.

And damn it if her body didn't respond. Her skin warmed up. He lungs squeezed tight. Her heart skipped a beat. "Screw him," she said, her voice soft, just for him. "Don't leave."

No, she hadn't just said that. But yes, she had. And she meant it. Because, despite telling herself it would be okay, that losing him was how it was meant to be, looking into the reality of watching him walk away was heart-breaking. She wasn't strong enough.

"Stay," she said again. "Stay."

Then she made the mistake of looking into Armand's eyes. And what she saw—the heady mix of desire and regret—made her want to weep.

He hadn't trusted her enough to include her in his concerns. That hurt. Now it was clear he didn't want her enough to even consider staying, years of abandonment fell in on her like walls in a demolished building.

She braced herself against the side of the chair as her knees gave way. Armand, being Armand, held out a hand to help her.

"I don't need your help, Armand. Or your protection. I'm tough, tougher than I look." And she was, she realised, as in a case of really wretched timing she felt her heart harden. "I'm an orphan. I'm farm stock. I'm educated. I'm capable. No matter what befalls me I will land on my feet because I say that I will."

"I know you will," he said, his accent, that warm, rough voice of his, nearly undoing her completely. "You are the strongest, sweetest, most fearless woman I have ever known."

*Then stay*, she begged inwardly; *fight for me. Love me.*

"While every time I let someone close they get hurt. If this doesn't show you that, I don't know what will. This is all my fault, Evie, and I cannot apologise to you enough."

He cared about her. He'd just said so. And she *knew* it. Deep down in that place that could read his eyes, his smiles, his tells, in a way she'd never been able to read another living soul. But to hear him say it took her knees out from under her.

"I care about you too," she said. "But for me, caring takes the form of sticking around. When anyone offers you attention, affection, love, you push them away, telling yourself it's because you're terrified that anyone who comes into contact with you would be poisoned by mere association. When the truth is, you're just terrified."

As tears burned the backs of her eyes, Evie moved around Armand and reached out a hand to Jonathon. "Thank you, Mr Montrose. For giving me a shot, for forcing me to take a risk and for teaching me a life lesson. Armand, it's been an education."

She grabbed her backpack, her beanie, her keyboard, and headed for the door.

"Take the rest of the day off, Ms Croft," said Jonathon. "You deserve it."

"I will, thanks. Because I need to find myself a new apartment. And a new job."

As she headed out the office door she heard Jonathon's murmur: "What just happened? I don't understand."

"She quit, you fool. That woman is the best thing that ever happened to your sorry soul and you never had a clue."

Jonathon's voice lifted as if shouting at a departing back as he said, "Maybe you should look in a mirror as you say those words."

When she heard footsteps following her, Evie ran down the stairs. Armand's strides were bigger; he caught up fast, taking her by the elbow, turning her to face him. "Evie. Don't do this."

"Which part?"

Mercury swirled behind his eyes, shifting with his mercurial thoughts. "Don't give up."

"Give up what? On us? On you?" She knew what he'd meant but she needed to hear him say it. For that connection that had drawn them to one another from that very first day made her refuse to believe he could simply let her go.

"Don't give up this opportunity. I warned you, that first day, that this place could eat you alive.

But now I know better. You would flourish here. Jonathon is a manipulative bastard, but he's the best there is. Use him. Whatever gig, whatever pay, whatever you want, it will be yours."

Evie reached out and gave him a shove. Then another. "I do not need Jonathon Montrose to get what I want. And if you can't see that…"

She'd risked, she'd leapt, she'd put herself further out on a limb than she'd ever intended. And she had fallen. Landed badly. And now felt broken—in her ego, in her head, in her heart, and seventeen other places besides.

She'd thought breaking the fortune's curse would set her free. Instead she'd banked her future on a mirage.

The other shoe had finally dropped.

She was done with this city. Done with trying to do the right thing and failing anyway.

As she walked out through the door and into the alleyway the bright, beautiful Melbourne winter's sky beaming down on her, she felt as if she was falling still.

There was only one place she could think of that would cushion her landing.

It was time to go home.

# CHAPTER TWELVE

THE RETIREMENT VILLAGE where Evie's grand-dad now lived was light, bright and inviting. No wind whistling through the old walls the way it had on the old farm. Central heating rather than a tetchy fireplace. And plenty of company of people his own age.

It must have been someone's birthday, as helium balloons bobbed about on the ceiling.

She spotted her granddad through the crowd the moment he spotted her.

"Evie, love!" he cried. "Christmas Evie. Happily Evie After." He came at her with a plate full of cake. And when she fell into her granddad's wiry hug she felt as though she could cry for a year.

"Come," he said. "Sit."

Evie came. She sat. Perched on the edge of a cool plastic chair. A table covered in paper plates, with half-eaten cake, scones and smatterings of cut soft fruit.

"Evie!" a woman called, and the word went around, "It's Evie."

She knew what they were after. She handed over her bag of beanies, and the women snapped them up, oohing and ahhing over the pom-poms, the cats' ears, the lurid colours.

Her granddad frowned at the stash. "Hope you haven't been spending all your spare time knitting for this lot."

"Hush," said one, giving him a nudge. And a smiling side eye. *Norma*, Evie thought, giving herself a mental note to ask about that later.

"Not all," Evie said. "I've been working a lot. Hanging out. Making new friends. Just like you wanted me to do."

"And Zoe?"

"Lance is back. For good. He's moved in with her, in fact. They are blissed out."

"Good for them. And you, Evie, love," said Granddad. "Have you found yourself a nice young man who…blisses you out?"

Evie smiled even while her heart throbbed painfully. "I didn't come here to talk about me, I came here to talk about you. And the latest JD Robb. How good was it?"

She'd dropped the magic word and now her table mates were off and running.

Soothing her with their touches on the hand. Quieting her pain with their ribald jokes. Easing her mind that, while she'd left her granddad behind, he was doing just fine. Better, even, than she'd ever imagined.

It gave her the tiniest kernel of hope she could one day feel that way too.

Not today.

But one day.

Borrowing her granddad's ancient truck, she swung by the farm.

She waved to Farmer Steve, son of their closest neighbour, who now rented the farm. He'd offered to buy her out, more than once. She told herself she'd kept it so her granddad could know that he'd left out of choice, not because she and his doctors had pushed.

But as she pulled up to the old farmhouse she knew. She'd kept it for herself. A back-up plan. A reason not to give herself completely to the Melbourne experiment in case it all went belly-up.

"Evie," Steve called, heading over to the fence, cattle dog in tow.

She hopped out of the truck and gave the dog a quick pat. "How's things?"

"You know."

She did. The life of a farmer was a difficult one.

"You staying?" he said, nudging his chin towards the house. "Your old room is the guest room."

She hadn't actually planned anything beyond fleeing the city, but in the end she said, "Sure. That'd be great."

Evie slept like the dead, waking hours after the dairy farm had been up and at 'em. More proof she was a city girl now—her body clock clearly no longer on farm time.

By the time she sauntered out to the kitchen the wildlings were at school, Steve was out fixing fences and his wife, Stacey, had headed into work at the local supermarket. The logs in the old fireplace had burned down to embers.

There was a note on the old kitchen table.

*Eggs, bacon and fresh milk in the fridge. Warm your towel over the heating rod in the bathroom.*

She put some bread in the ancient toaster and while she waited for it to pop she took a quiet tour about her childhood home—finding the burn mark from when she'd discovered chemistry, the notches of her growth chart behind the pantry door. She'd passed her mother's height when she was thirteen.

As she slathered the hot toast in homemade butter and jam, she let herself wonder what it might be like if she decided to stay. She could teach senior citizens how to use the internet, fix computers, get contracts with the local schools to help out with their IT programs.

It was a beautiful town. Slow and quiet, lovely and dear. But it wasn't her home. Not any more.

Armand might have let her down but he had changed her too. With his deeply held sense of duty and love. His spirit of adventure. His bravery, his determination to stand up for what he thought was right.

There was no going back after that. No more cautiously hacking her way through the levels of her life—she wanted to meet it head-on. There would be bumps and bruises, there would be mistakes made. But that was okay. More than okay. More challenging. More engaging. More wonderful. For that was life.

And she wasn't going to go another day not living it.

Sticking the toast between her teeth, she grabbed the notepaper from the kitchen table and turned it over to scribble a note to Steve:

*If you want the farm, it's all yours.*

As soon as she wrote the words down she felt a sense of relief. Of letting go of the final shackles holding her back.

Now to figure out what it was she truly wanted so she could go out and get it.

Top of that list: Hot Stuff in the Swanky Suit.

For Armand was her "it" and had been from the moment she'd set eyes on him. And she was his. He might have taken longer to realise it—because he was stubborn and brooding and a man—but she knew he felt it too.

He'd told her so. In his own way.

But, while he claimed he was no hero, he felt it was up to him to fix everything, save everyone, all on his own. When things went wrong he shouldered all the blame. That was why he'd let her go. Not because he didn't care, but because he did.

All she had to do was make him see he wasn't alone any more. She'd be there, backing him up, patching him up, holding his hand, listening, caring right on back.

She'd been too scared to look for her life's passion, but she'd found it anyway.

She moved to the height chart and placed a kiss on her mother's last notch, then took one last turn about the farm kitchen to say goodbye.

Now what? Evie turned right, then left, like a chicken with its head chopped off.

*Stop. Think. Finish breakfast, put on clothes, get the car back to Granddad and head to the city.*

Wrapping herself in a blanket off the back of a couch, she bit down on her toast and stepped out onto the porch to see if she could see Steve out in the field to let him know she was heading off, when...

She choked, spraying crumbs all over her clothes. "Armand?"

Armand looked up at the sound of his name, his shiny brogues stopping halfway up the farmhouse stairs, his gaze travelling over her as if making sure what he was seeing was true. Or maybe it was her wild bed-hair, old brown blanket and scuzzy old Ugg boots that had him transfixed.

"How did you find me?" she asked, mind scrambled, senses in a tizz.

While, in his elegant chinos, button-down shirt and cashmere sweater, he looked the picture of cool. Only his eyes gave him away, all tempestuous stormy blue and focussed on her like a laser beam. "I asked Zoe, but even after using extensive torture techniques she didn't budge."

"And you with all your training."

At her sass a spark lit within the stormy depths of Armand's eyes.

Her voice was husky as she said, "Jonathon."

"He owed me. He went to HR. Your granddad is your next of kin. The farm is his address."

"Your friend has no respect for propriety."

"For which I am extremely grateful."

Evie took another step forward. Then, caught in the man's magnetic pull, she stepped forward again.

A muscle worked in Armand's jaw as he took the final step up onto the porch so Evie had to tilt her chin. He looked...tired, fraught and beautiful.

Evie hitched the blanket up. Curled her toes into her socks. Asked, "Why are you here?"

"You know why," he said, that accent sending delicious shivers down her spine.

And okay, maybe she did. Because she was smart and he wasn't a man to make empty gestures. Yet her heart thumped hard enough against her ribs that it knocked her forwards a step.

Right as Armand reached out to wrap an arm about her waist, haul her to him and kiss her.

Evie threw her arms around his neck and kissed him right on back.

*This*, she thought. *This is what life is all about.*

Then she didn't think much at all for quite some time.

When Evie pulled back she breathed deeply of the chill farm air, of Armand. The feel of him filling her with warmth, with hope, with bliss.

*I'm blissed out, Granddad!* she thought. Already looking forward to introducing her two favourite men in the world.

With a sigh she tipped up onto her toes, wrapped her arms around Armand and buried her face in his neck. Then tossed the toast still gripped in her cold fingers out onto the dry grass, the chickens and ducks squawking as they swarmed to tear it apart.

"Evie," said Armand as she looked up into his eyes, "I should have told you the moment I realised what Jonathon had done."

"You should. But you thought you were protecting me, which is a nice thing to think. Next time know that including me is nicer still."

"Next time?"

"Yes, please."

He kissed her again, on the tip of the nose. On the edge of her eye. On her mouth. Marking his place.

"I truly wanted to kill Jonathon for putting us

through all that. Yet at the same time I feel like I should hug him for putting us through all that."

Armand smiled against her mouth before sealing it with a long, knee-melting kiss. "An urge I have had to subdue more times than you can count. The killing part, not the hugging."

"I can count pretty high."

"And yet..."

Evie shivered at the rough note in Armand's voice. To stave off more shivers, she found the edges of the blanket and wrapped them around him too.

"Now," he said, "I have a question for you."

"Bring it on."

"Did you come here because you finally realised dairy farming was your life's dream?"

Evie laughed. "I did not."

"Excellent. And what about working for Jonathon? I know he is putting together an extremely generous proposal in the hopes of luring you back."

"Been there," she said. "Done that."

"I'm glad, because the conversation we had about following curiosity stuck. And I have an idea that I hope piques yours."

"I'm finally going to be a bus driver? No ballerina firefighter!"

"If that is your dream then I support it whole-heartedly. If you are teasing me, then I have a generous offer of my own."

"I'm teasing you. Offer away."

"How would you feel about working for me?"

"For you, or with you?"

Armand's smile was quick and bright and glorious. And gave nothing away. "I'm setting up an Australian office."

"Of your company? The Action Adventure All-Stars? You're getting the band back together!"

"In a way. Only this time I would like to be proactive rather than reactive."

"Okay."

"Much of the planning happened on my trip up here on the train, so the details are sketchy at best. But how would you feel about helping me design safety apps for commuters travelling at night? For starters. Apps for travellers; how to be aware, safety conscious. Self-defence class apps. The sky is the limit. You could have your own team, hand-picked, with the side benefit of doing work that makes the world a better place. What do you think?"

Evie wondered if it was possible to smile from the bottoms of your feet to the top of your head, because that was what it felt like. "I think you only kissed me to soften me up to get me to work for you." She also thought he was wonderful. "If so you're sneakier than Jonathon ever was."

When Armand's brows lowered and his smile took on a predatory gleam the feeling rushing about in her body was far more fun than a mere smile.

"I didn't come all this way to offer you a job. I came all this way to offer you a life. My life. With all that that means. I know I am flawed, and stubborn, and struggle to ask for help."

"You are also generous. Astute. Forgiving. Loyal. Steadfast. And devastatingly handsome."

He pulled her closer and her entire body sighed. "Taking all that into account, I hope that you can take me as I am."

"I'll take you any way I can get you." Evie lifted a hand to swipe the hair from Armand's eyes.

"You have no idea how glad I am to hear you say that." He breathed in, his eyes travelling slowly over her face as if he couldn't believe what he was seeing. "That moment—when I thought you were about to leap onto the train tracks— my life literally flashed before my eyes. A life in which you were no more. Every horror I had witnessed in my life coalesced into a ball of lead inside me and I could not get the image out of my head."

*Oh, Armand.*

He went on. "After you left—no, after I pushed you away—I had every intention of going back to Paris, deliberately choosing the fugue in which I had been existing, as it seemed a lesser evil than a life without you. Until I realised the thing I had feared most had—in its own way—happened anyway. You would be gone to me. I would never see you again. And it was my fault."

Evie opened her mouth to contradict him, to admit to her own part in the whole mess, but he leaned down and pressed his forehead to hers and her words dried up in her mouth.

"I love you, Evie. And the thought of life without you is no life at all. I want you with all the risk and joy you bring. And I came here hoping to convince you to give me a second chance."

Evie could barely breathe. Her heart was full, her mind reeling, her blood singing in her veins because of this big, strong man with his grand, poetic heart.

Evie smiled, then grinned, then laughed. Rubbing her forehead against his, she said, "Armand, I've been a little bit in love with you since you were no more to me than my train boyfriend, Hot

Stuff in the Swanky Suit. Now that I know you, the real you, flesh and blood and heart and soul, I love you with everything I have."

She felt Armand's body shift as if with shock.

He lifted away, to look into her eyes, his own swirling with emotion. Before they narrowed. "I thought I was Reading Guy."

"That's right. You were Reading Guy. Why am I telling all this to you?"

She made to pull away before he wrapped her up tight.

His mouth kicked up at one side. He had a hell of a smile when he let it loose. "I can go one better, *ma chérie*. I have loved you longer still. Since before we even met."

"Oh, really?"

"Picture the darkest, roughest, farthest reaches of the planet. My spent body protesting every movement, my exhausted mind struggling to form coherent thought, I looked up one night to find the sky awash with more stars than I had ever seen before. And in that darkness, not knowing if any of us would survive the night, I prayed that somewhere in the world a woman had looked to those same stars. A woman whose joy and determination, quirks and kindness and light could fill the very edges of the darkness."

Evie didn't even know she was crying until Armand brushed the pad of a thumb over her cheek.

This time she kissed him, sinking against the long, strong lines of his body as she loved him with all her heart.

"You are my girl in the stars, Evie. My counterpoint. My way out of the dark. The Girl with the Perfect Aim who got me right through the heart. This is the day my life truly begins. No games. No rules. And I want to spend every day of that life with you."

Evie didn't have to think, overthink, or think twice. "Yes, yes, yes, yes, *yes!*"

"That's a yes?"

"Yes!"

Grinning, indulgently, Armand squeezed her tighter still, lifting her feet off the ground. Then he spun her about until she laughed so hard she could scarcely catch her breath, the sound carrying off into the sharp, wintry sky.

"Then let's get the hell out of here," he said.

Evie nodded. "Let's go home."

# EPILOGUE

EVIE SAT ON the train heading into the city, giving into the rock and roll of the carriage.

It had been three months since that day at the farm, when Armand had literally swept her off her feet. It had been a whirlwind since.

She'd gone back to Zoe's, packed her things and spent a week of sleepovers there to unravel their living arrangements and to say goodbye to their single-girl days together.

Then she'd moved her one bag of stuff to Armand's—leaving the futon behind.

Together they'd gone to see Jonathon. She'd thanked him properly for the opportunity and told him she had found a position more suited to her skills. A bittersweet moment, to be sure.

Though watching Armand demand free space in Jonathon's building for the Australian offices of the Action Adventure All-Stars—not their real name—had been far more fun. He was a keen negotiator—all spit and fire while cool as ice. She banked it for future alone time.

Armand could afford to buy his own building, but the demand was down to his innate sense of justice. And Jonathon had acquiesced, appearing honestly chagrined at the part he'd played in deceiving them both.

Emphasis on the "appearing", as when they'd left the office Evie had looked back to see him puffing out his chest and looking well pleased with himself. Jonathon was a manipulative bastard, but thankfully he was their manipulative bastard.

And now she really did have the best job ever—heading up the cyber-security division of Armand's company. She had staff—and what do you know, it was really easy to find plenty of super-smart, super-talented, IT-savvy women to work for her. Once Armand had met Lance—who'd just left his position in the army—he'd offered him a job on the spot too.

"Do you have enough room?" Armand asked, shifting to give her more space.

Evie ate up the inches, snuggling closer. She sneaked her hand into the crook of Armand's arm and leant her head on his shoulder. Her eyes slid over the frazzled mother, the schoolboys with their huge bags and glazed eyes, the suits and the yoga queens and the grinders and the hipsters. All of them on a mission to live their best lives—all dealing as best they could with the hiccups and detours and falls and successes along the way.

Evie smiled at them all, each and every one of them helping to make this city of hers the vibrant melting pot of possibility that it was.

"Look."

At the rumble of Armand's voice Evie turned to look at him. The storm in his eyes had cleared, making way for acres of blue. A glint shone within as he took her by the chin and turned her head away. "Over there."

Another couple sat a couple of rows down, all snuggled up too. A young man with short blond hair and Harry Potter glasses was reading from a small hardcover book to a girl with tufts of short dark hair poking out at the bottom of a navy beanie covered in little gold stars, and a big, soppy smile on her face.

Evie wondered about the knitting pattern. Machine-made, perhaps? Those stars would be seriously challenging to...

She sat bolt upright.

Then let go of Armand to grab her phone. She frantically found the app she was looking for and scrolled back weeks, months, till she found the right page. Then she stuck it under Armand's nose, listening with half an ear as he read:

*New to your orbit, I find myself struck*
*By your raven locks, your starlit eyes. What*
*luck*
*That I find myself able to see you twice a day.*
*A beacon in a sea of strangers. I must say*
*Your sunshine smiles are my good morning.*
*Your evening sighs my goodnight.*
*If I had the courage I'd say hello.*
*Till then I remain alone in my delight.*

"Well, what do you know?" said Armand.

*Not much*, thought Evie, *clearly.*

"Funny," he said, giving her a sideways glance as he handed back her phone. "One could think it was written about you."

Evie merely smiled and gave him a quick kiss.

He'd found the fortune cookie message scrunched up in her wallet when he'd gone looking for coins and he'd listened with impressive patience while she'd talked him through the story that went along with it.

They'd get to the poem in good time. But not yet. Armand had taught her that a little mystery could go a long way.

How funny though, she thought, all the external forces that had worked to get them together. The dodgy fortune, someone else's poem and an unlikely fairy godfather in the shape of Jonathon Montrose.

But the truth was they had found one another on the train before any of that had even come to pass. Harbouring quiet fascinations for one another while at points in their lives where the idea of love at first sight was too momentous a leap to believe in.

"Would you like me to read to you?" he asked.

"Depends what you are reading, Reading Guy," Evie said, knowing he could read the back of a cereal box and that voice of his would make her knees quiver.

He pulled out the book he'd tucked inside his coat—*Cyrano de Bergerac*.

"In French?" she asked.

"Of course," he said, taken aback that she would suggest otherwise.

"I thought you read fiction to keep your language skills up to scratch."

"I read fiction because it exists."

"Armand Debussey, you're a romantic."

"That is like telling me I am French," he said, with not a lick of irony.

Evie realised she'd only scratched the surface of this man. That his code went deep. And, while she had the feeling he could be the one project she might never fully crack, that was okay with her. She'd have a wonderful time trying.

\* \* \* \* \*

# LET'S TALK
# Romance

For exclusive extracts, competitions and special offers, find us online:

**f** facebook.com/millsandboon

**⊙** @millsandboonuk

**𝕏** @millsandboon

Or get in touch on 0844 844 1351*

For all the latest titles coming soon, visit millsandboon.co.uk/nextmonth